Toby

Toby

BY ART WALLACE

ILLUSTRATED BY
JANE ARMSTRONG WALWORTH

DOUBLEDAY & COMPANY, INC.,
GARDEN CITY, NEW YORK

Library of Congress Catalog Card Number 70–166421
Copyright © 1971 by Art Wallace

Printed in the United States of America
First Edition

S 5

*for
Soni,
Sheila,
and
Baron*

Toby

Chapter One:
The Phantoms
of the Fourth Grade

Zoom! Over the crest of the hill they come, legs pumping hard, bodies hunched low, eyes squinting against the early morning sun. Zoom! Zoom! Zoom! There are three of them charging down the slope, grinning their Saturday grins, smiling their nine-year-old-boy-on-a-bicycle smiles.

Saturday! Absolutely and without question the best day of the week. No school today, and when today is over then there's no school tomorrow, either. And what could be better than that?

"No hands! Pass it on!" yells Joe Rooney, spreading his arms out wide, balancing on his shiny two-wheeler like a bird about to fly halfway to Kansas City and back.

"No hands!" yells Harry Kurawicz, following Joe's lead, coasting happily down the hill, hands stretching out as far as they can go.

"No hands!" echoes Mike Rizzo, pushing his glasses firmly up on the bridge of his nose, raising his hands gingerly from the handle bars, and then gripping them again tightly as his bike begins to swerve. Mike can't quite make it, but he doesn't care. Nothing and no one could spoil this day.

Nothing could spoil this happy, sunshiny, Octobery, gleeful, joyful, marvelous day.

Down the slope they ride, around the curve into Center Street, pedaling up onto the sidewalk, around parked cars, and right through the pile of leaves Mr. Cooper has just carefully gathered on his front lawn.

"Come back here, you kids!" screams Mr. Cooper, the veins standing out angrily on his fat neck. "Come back here!" he cries, waving his rake furiously in their direction. The boys grin, wave back, and disappear around the corner into Elm Street.

Maybe Mr. Cooper will remember them now. Maybe he won't be so quick to chase the Phantoms of the Fourth Grade away from their very own swimming hole, just so he can go fishing on a Saturday afternoon.

Besides, it wouldn't hurt Mr. Cooper to do a little more raking. He's much fatter than he should be, and Joe's grandfather is always talking about how being too heavy can shorten a man's life.

As a matter of fact, maybe they're doing Mr. Cooper a favor.

"The supermarket!" Joe yells. "Pass it on!"

"The supermarket!" yells Harry, wondering what Joe has in mind.

"The supermarket!" echoes Mike, pushing his glasses once more up onto the bridge of his nose.

They pedal rapidly toward the huge parking lot of the Carlyle Supermarket with Joe in the lead, as always. And why not? When a boy can ride a bike better, hit a baseball farther, climb a rope higher, hold his breath under water longer, and wiggle his toes faster than any other kid in the fourth grade, then he's bound to be the leader.

And Joe Rooney can do all these things.

Up into the supermarket parking lot, circle a few shopping carts, and zoom around to the loading area in the back. Joe in the lead, Harry and Mike trailing along behind, like the tail of a kite on wheels. The Phantoms of the Fourth Grade are still on the march!

Joe's target this time is Horrible Homer Lippincott, the most loud-mouthed, sour-tempered, kid-chasing stock clerk who ever worked at the Carlyle Supermarket. For instance, only last Saturday afternoon Joe, Harry, and Mike had offered to help Homer Lippincott carry a crate of eggs into the store. Had Horrible Homer thanked them for their kindness? Absolutely not. Had he yelled at them and called them names and threatened to send for the manager if they didn't leave him alone? That was exactly what he did.

Had he even thrown rotten tomatoes at them? Well, just ask Mike what his mother said when he came home with that big red stain all over his nice new shirt!

The boys round the corner of the supermarket. Joe grins. Not only is Horrible Homer in the loading area, but he's unloading crates of oranges from a truck. And not only is he unloading crates of oranges from a truck, but he's just dropped one, and is busily bending down trying to pick up the oranges that are rolling all over the ground.

"Follow the leader!" yells Joe. He pedals forward, right at the startled stock clerk. And before Horrible Homer can even think about throwing a rotten tomato, Joe has bent down, scooped up an orange, and zoomed off without slowing down at all.

"Hey, you!" Homer shouts. "Come . . . !" But he never even finishes his sentence, as Harry now speeds by, bending down and picking up an orange. And then Mike does the same, almost losing his glasses in the process.

This is too much! Horrible Homer chases out into the loading area after them. "Come back here!" he yells. "Bring that fruit back!"

"We're only helping you pick them up, Mr. Lippincott!" Joe calls out, holding an orange high over his head.

"We're only trying to be helpful, Mr. Lippincott!" Harry shouts, tossing an orange up and down as he rides along.

"That's right, Mr. Lippincott!" Mike yells, trying to keep an orange in his hand and his glasses on his nose at the same time.

"Bring that fruit back!" Homer repeats, almost jumping up and down in his rage, his face gradually becoming the color of a tomato stain on a boy's nice new shirt.

"Bring that fruit back!" he cries again, as the boys circle around him on their bikes, grinning and holding their oranges high enough in the air so Homer will be sure to see them.

"Bring that fruit back!" he screams, as the waiting truck drivers lean against their trucks, nudge each other, and smile.

"Yes, sir, Mr. Lippincott!" Joe finally answers. He pedals his bike in a wide circle, Harry and Mike following close behind. "Charge!" he shouts, as he heads his bike directly toward the suddenly frightened stock clerk.

Homer's eyes bulge out. He can't believe it. These crazy kids are going to run him down! Closer and closer Joe comes, grinning all the time. Closer and closer, until Homer is ready to run for his life. Closer and closer, until Joe swerves to one side, tosses the orange, and yells, "Catch!"

Homer fumbles, desperately trying to hold the orange.

But then Harry tosses an orange to him, and then Mike. Horrible Homer may be many things, but he is certainly not a good juggler, and those three oranges go bouncing around in his arms like rubber balls against a concrete wall. He twists and he turns and he struggles and he stretches, but all those oranges go plop-plop-plopping to the ground. And right on top of them, losing his balance, plops Homer.

The boys can hear the truck drivers laughing at Homer as they ride off. They know that if there's one thing a loud-mouthed, sour-tempered, kid-chasing grownup can't stand, it's to have other grownups watch three nine-year-old kids get the better of him.

They almost feel sorry for Homer.

Almost.

Not quite.

Zoom! Zoom! Zoom! Down the street they ride, around the corner, past the church, over the bridge, through the alley, and out into Columbus Street. Every small town in Kansas has a street that's a little bit wider, where the houses are a little bit bigger, where the lawns are a little bit fancier, where the bike racing is a little bit better.

"On your mark!" shouts Joe, waiting for Harry and Mike to come up alongside him.

"Get set!" yells Harry, bending low over the handle bars.

"Go!" cries Mike, hoping he'll win a race for at least once in his life.

Pedaling with all their might, the Phantoms of the Fourth Grade speed down Columbus Street. They speed past the parked cars, the elegant houses, the fancy lawns, and the biggest moving van they've ever seen in their lives.

Moving van???!!

That's what it is, all right. A great big eight-wheeled

red and yellow giant, parked in front of 975 Columbus Street. Not only that, but the lawn in front of the red brick house is dotted with cartons and barrels and chairs and all sorts of odds and ends. And not only that, but two broad-shouldered moving men are busily carrying a dining room table through the front door.

A bicycle race is fun, but you can do that any old day. How many times do you get the chance to help moving men carry things into a house? That's even more fun than riding through Mr. Cooper's pile of leaves or helping Horrible Homer collect his oranges. And besides, they all know that Joe would win the race anyway. He always does.

The three boys describe a wide circle in the street and pedal back to the moving van. Coming to a halt beside its yawning doors, they straddle their bikes and gape at the furniture still waiting to be unloaded.

"They sure have a lot of stuff," Joe says, thinking of the fun of helping the moving men carry the living room sofa.

"I wonder if they'll want the Carlyle *Bee,*" Harry says, thinking of the weekly newspaper he delivers early every Thursday morning.

"I guess they don't have any kids," Mike says, noticing that there aren't any baseball bats or tennis rackets or ice skates or toys of any kind.

They turn and stare at the house. They see the worn red brick, they see the rose trellises, they see the freshly painted white window frames. They see all these things, but they miss what is most important. What they don't see is the face.

The face belongs to a nine-year-old boy standing in one of the bare rooms of the newly-bought house and peering out at the Phantoms of the Fourth Grade. Fair haired, brown eyed, neither tall nor short, neither fat nor thin, he secretly watches the three boys straddling their bikes near the moving van, studying them, wondering who they are.

He'd wonder even more, if he knew he was going to lead them into one of the most frightening adventures of their lives.

His name is Toby.

Chapter Two:
Enter Toby

His full name is Tobias Spencer Hammond, and at this moment he almost wishes his father hadn't been promoted to head the research department of the new electronics plant here in Carlyle, Kansas. He wishes they hadn't had to move.

Most of all, he wishes he could still be sitting in the comfortable living room of their apartment in New York City, instead of standing at the window of this strange house, watching three boys near a moving van, and wondering if they will want to be friends with him.

The Phantoms of the Fourth Grade still straddle their bicycles, watching as the weary moving men climb up into the van and prepare to carry an eight-foot sofa into the house.

"Can we help, mister?" Joe asks hopefully.

"Just stay out of the way, kids," says the moving man with the big mustache.

"We could carry some of the little stuff for you," suggests Harry.

"Can't you understand English?" growls the sweaty moving man with the bald head. "He told you to stay out of the way."

"All we want to do is help," says Mike nervously, determined not to be left out of the discussion.

The two moving men look at each other. One wipes the sweat from his bald head, while the other tugs wearily at his big mustache.

"Go ride your bikes," sighs Mustache.

"And leave us alone," pleads Bald Head, adding fiercely, "unless you want us to drop this eight-foot sofa on your heads."

Toby watches all this from the window, wishing he were the kind of boy who could just walk up to other kids and smile and say "Hi" and be friends, just like that. Moving to a new town can be an exciting adventure, but it can also be frightening. You have to go to a new school, and you have to make new friends, and if the kids don't like you, you can end up being the loneliest nine-year-old boy in the world.

"I don't care," Toby mutters to himself as he stands by the window. "I don't even care if they hate me."

That's when he crosses to the front door, takes a deep breath, hopes he won't say the wrong thing the way he usually does, and walks slowly toward the van.

Joe Rooney is the first to see him. "Hi," he says, wondering where this new boy has come from.

Toby is too nervous to answer. He simply looks at Joe, then at Harry, and then at Mike.

"Hi," says Harry Kurawicz.

"Hi," says Mike Rizzo, adding, "My name's Mike."

Toby finally manages to smile. "Hi," he answers.

"You moving in here?" asks Joe.

"Uh-huh," Toby says. Then he turns to the moving men, who are about to carry the sofa into the house. "Be careful of my Geiger counter. It's in one of the cartons on the truck."

"Don't sweat, sonny," grunts the sweaty man with the bald head.

"What's a Gieger counter?" Mike asks as the moving men carry the sofa toward the front door.

"Something I built," Toby says.

"What does it do?" Joe wants to know.

"You wouldn't understand if I told you," Toby replies.

"Why?" Joe says, beginning to be annoyed. "You think I'm stupid?"

"You said that. I didn't."

"I bet you don't know yourself," Joe challenges angrily. "I bet you made the whole thing up."

By now Toby knows he has done just what he had hoped he wouldn't do. Instead of stepping up and smiling and saying "Hi" and being friends, he had been smart-alecky and show-offy and just plain nasty. And there isn't a kid in the world who likes a smart-alecky, show-offy nine-year-old, even if he does happen to be almost a genius.

And that's what Toby is, all right. Almost a genius. Back home in New York City he had been tested by doctors with long beards and questioned by doctors with thick spectacles, and they had decided that any boy who can beat his brilliant father at chess, who can build a complicated instrument like a Geiger counter, who can do difficult arithmetic problems in his head, and who can read and understand serious grown-up books is certainly a lot smarter than an ordinary boy.

Poor Toby. Sometimes it's hard to be almost a genius,

especially when all you really want to do is be friends with three strange boys in a new town. But now they're all staring at him angrily, waiting to see how he will answer Joe.

"Of course I know what a Geiger counter is. I built it, didn't I?" Toby finally says. "A Geiger counter happens to be an instrument for detecting radioactivity."

"That's just what I thought it was," Joe says, determined not to let this show-offy kid get the better of him.

"If you're so smart, what's radioactivity?" challenges Toby.

"If *you* don't know, why should *I* tell you," retorts Joe. Then he turns to Harry and Mike and says, "Come on, fellers." And before Toby can even have a chance to think of an answer, all three boys hop on their bikes and zoom away.

Zoom! Zoom! Zoom! Off they go, down Columbus Street, and all Toby can do is yell as loudly as he can. "You *are* stupid!" he shouts. "You don't know anything!" he screams.

And all the time, he's wishing they would come back so he could tell them he's sorry.

Chapter Three:
Toby-Shmoby!

"Toby! Toby, where are you?"

Toby doesn't even hear his mother's voice as he stands in front of the house, still watching the three boys riding their bikes down Columbus Street.

"Toby!" his mother calls again. "Lunch is ready!"

Lunch. The last thing he wants now is lunch. What he really wants is a magic carpet or a racing car or a jet that would zoom him away from here and back to New York faster than a rocket headed for the moon. But since he doesn't have any of those things, all he can do is turn around and walk slowly back toward his house to lunch.

Toby isn't the only one who turns. "Follow the leader!" Joe shouts as he wheels his bike around in a circle and races back up Columbus Street. Harry and Mike follow close behind.

"No hands!" shouts Joe, wanting to show Toby how talented he is.

"No hands!" echoes Harry, flinging his arms out to the wind.

"No hands!" cries Mike, hoping he'll be able to do it this time.

In spite of himself, Toby turns to watch the Phantoms of the Fourth Grade as they glide by like three happy eagles flying over a mountaintop. And at that moment he would rather be able to ride a bike with no hands than answer all the questions of all the doctors with long beards and thick spectacles.

"Toby!" his mother calls for the third time. "Come inside! Toby!"

Once again Toby turns, and once again Harry and Mike follow close behind Joe as he pedals around in a circle. Up on the sidewalk he goes, feet churning, hair blowing, mouth grinning, moving closer and closer to the unsuspecting boy.

"Toby-Shmoby!" Joe singsongs, as he swerves to one side at the last second and circles around the startled Toby.

"Toby-Shmoby!" chant Harry and Mike, following Joe's lead as they always do.

"Toby-Shmoby! Toby-Shmoby! Toby-Shmoby!" they all sing as they circle around and around the frightened boy. "Toby-Shmoby! Toby-Shmoby! Toby-Shmoby!"

Toby turns this way and that way, desperate to escape the prison of spinning wheels and pedaling feet and grinning faces and chanting voices that surround him as if he were the center of a giant dart board.

"Toby-Shmoby! Toby-Shmoby! Toby-Shmoby!" they sing gleefully.

Whirling, spinning, pressing against his ears. Chanting, laughing, making him want to scream. Around and around, tormenting, stinging, mocking.

"TOBY-SHMOBY! TOBY-SHMOBY! TOBY-SHMOBY!"

He closes his eyes and clamps his hands over his ears. Anything to shut out the sound of those hated voices, voices that suddenly grow fainter, voices that trail behind the Phantoms of the Fourth Grade as they cycle happily off down the street.

Toby opens his eyes and groans. Then he does what he usually does. "I don't care," he mutters to himself again. "I don't even care if they hate me."

His tormentors are gone at last, and Toby turns to enter the house, almost bumping into Bald Head and Mustache as they come out to get more furniture. "Hey, genius," says Bald Head. "Your mother's been calling you."

Toby scowls at them, ignoring their grins, and picks his way through the cartons scattered on the living room floor. He bends down beside his father, who is trying to sort out the hundreds of books they had brought with them.

"Want to pick out which books are yours," asks Mr. Hammond, "and put them in your room?"

But Toby isn't in the mood for sorting books. And he has a great many of them. Books on astronomy and geology and history and philosophy and dozens of other brain-dazzling subjects that made those long-bearded doctors sit up and wonder. "I wish we could've stayed in New York," he says.

"Give the town a chance," his father says. "You'll like it here."

"I hate it here," Toby says.

"So there you are," says Toby's mother, coming into the room carrying a sandwich on a paper plate. "I've been calling you. I fixed you a sandwich."

"I'm not hungry."

"Where have you been?" his mother asks.

"Outside," Toby answers, picking up one of his philosophy books. "I was talking to some kids."

"You mean you've made friends already? Why, that's wonderful!" She smiles at Toby's father, who isn't smiling at all. Instead, he is looking worriedly at his son, thinking of the problems a boy can have when he moves to a strange town.

"What about school?" Toby suddenly asks. "Do all the kids in this town go to the same school?"

"Of course they do," his mother answers. "You'll be in the fourth grade with all the other nine-year-olds. Why?"

"Just wondering," Toby shrugs.

Today is Saturday, he thinks. Tomorrow is Sunday, and then comes Monday. And there's nothing anybody can do to stop Monday from coming, no matter how much he wishes he could.

For Monday means going to school. Not only that, but it means going to the same school that Joe, Harry, and Mike go to. Probably the same class.

Toby doesn't look forward to that at all.

Not one bit.

"Toby," his father says quietly, "I told you to give the town a chance. Well, there's more." He puffs on his pipe and looks at his son earnestly. "Give the kids a chance, too."

Chapter Four:
It's Toby-Shmoby
Pass it on

Screaming, yelling, shouting, talking, giggling, laughing, whistling, burping, singing, running, ball-throwing, frisbee-tossing, jacks-playing, rope-skipping. The Carlyle Elementary School is a red-brick building surrounded by noise.

"Gosh, a whole week of questions and tests and teachers giving homework," groans Joe Rooney as he tosses a ball to his friends.

"Oh, me. A whole week of questions and tests and boys throwing spitballs," sighs Miss Phillips, the fourth grade teacher, as she stands in the playground watching the bedlam around her. It is almost eight-thirty on Monday morning, and in just a few minutes another week of school will begin.

Miss Phillips is forty-five years old. She has bright red hair and freckles and a nose too big for her face. She has a squeaky voice and a habit of squinting her eyes when one of her students does something to annoy her. She likes lemon meringue pie and neatly dressed girls and boys who don't throw spitballs. She hates chocolate ice cream and show-offs and children who don't do their homework.

At exactly half-past eight the first bell rings. Miss Phillips sighs one more sigh and starts one more day. "All right, line up!" she squeaks. "Fourth grade, line up!"

All around her, other teachers are calling out to other grades, but Miss Phillips is only interested in the thirty-one students in the fourth grade, who are starting to form a straggling line in the playground.

Most of all, she is interested in Joe Rooney. Not only is Joe Rooney one of the busiest spitball-throwers in the class, but right now he is still tossing the ball up in the air as he walks slowly and unhappily toward the line of boys and girls.

Miss Phillips squints her eyes. "Come on, Joseph. Hurry up."

"Yes, ma'am," Joe answers, so sweetly that everyone knows he is just trying to be funny. All his friends giggle. And that means all the kids, because Joe is certainly the most popular boy in the fourth grade.

"All right," Miss Phillips says sternly, "we're not moving one step until everyone is quiet."

"All right," Joe says, squinting his eyes and imitating Miss Phillips, "we're not moving one step until everyone is quiet." Of course, he doesn't say it out loud. Even Joe wouldn't dare do that. But he moves his lips and wiggles his head just the way Miss Phillips does, and the kids who can see him start giggling all over again.

Poor Miss Phillips. She has the same trouble almost every morning, when all she really wants to do is get her students into school so she can teach them reading and arithmetic and history and geography, so they can grow up and be lawyers and doctors and Presidents of the United States.

"Hey, look!" Harry whispers suddenly, pointing toward the entrance to the schoolyard.

"Who is it?" whispers a skinny boy named Sam Plover.

"Toby-Shmoby," answers Joe, as he watches Toby and his mother crossing the schoolyard. "I told you about him. Remember?"

Sam grins and turns to the fat boy next to him. "It's Toby-Shmoby," he whispers. "Pass it on."

Up and down the fourth grade line the words are whispered over and over again. "It's Toby-Shmoby. Pass it on." By the time Toby and his mother have reached the entrance to the school building, he can tell that everyone in the fourth grade is looking at him.

There's hardly anything as terrible for a nine-year-old boy as starting a strange new school with a bunch of kids who have known each other for years. And it's even worse for Toby, because he's sure he's made enemies even before his first day.

Across the schoolyard, in his clean white shirt, neatly pressed trousers, brightly shined shoes. Across the school-yard, trying to pretend he doesn't see the fourth grade staring at him. Across the schoolyard, feeling their eyes digging into the back of his head.

Maybe I'm just imagining it, he thinks as he reaches the main entrance with his mother. Maybe they don't hate me at all. Maybe if I turn and look, I'll see them all grinning and waving and shouting they're glad to have me in their class.

He turns and he looks and he listens. But he doesn't see grins and he doesn't hear shouts of welcome. What he does see are the boys and girls of the fourth grade staring at him as if he were a fly about to be swatted. And what he hears is his mother calling to him. "Come on, Toby," she says. "Let's go inside."

"I'll show them," he says to himself as he follows his mother into the school. "I'll show them how smart I am."

And he will.

Chapter Five:
36 times 27

"As you can see, this is multiplication with a two-place multiplier," says Miss Phillips as she writes multiplication problems on the blackboard.

If there's anything Miss Phillips hates more than chocolate ice cream, it's writing on the blackboard. Because that's when she has to turn her back to the class, and that's when boys like Joe Rooney start throwing spitballs.

But Joe isn't interested in spitballs right now. He isn't interested in multiplication problems, either. Instead, seated at his desk in the middle of the fourth grade classroom, he is very busy drawing a picture on a piece of notepaper.

"Joseph Rooney!"

Joe looks up and sees what he hates to see. He sees Miss Phillips staring right at him, squinting her angriest squint, pursing her lips, gripping her chalk, shaking her head, and pointing her long finger at the sketch on his desk.

"Since you have been paying such close attention," she says in a voice that sounds like chalk rubbing against a blackboard, "I'm sure you won't mind standing up and telling us how to do the first problem." She points to the blackboard. "36 times 27."

"36 times 27?" he gulps, wishing he had done his home-work over the weekend.

"That's right, Joseph," Miss Phillips replies as the whole class watches and hopes Joe will know the answer.

"36 times 27," Joe says again as he rises to his feet. "36 times 27," he repeats, wishing he could say it over and over again until the bell rings ending the period.

Miss Phillips knows most of the tricks a nine-year-old boy might try. "We know the problem, Joseph," she says. "What we want is the answer."

"Well, I . . . what I mean is, you take the . . . I think you multiply . . ." He probably could have gone on forever if the door hadn't opened and Mr. Samson, the assistant principal, hadn't come in just then with Toby at his side.

"All right, Joseph," Miss Phillips says. "I'll get back to you later." Joe sits down quickly, as Miss Phillips turns to Mr. Samson to see what trouble he is bringing her this time.

Brow furrowed, tongue protruding from between his lips, pencil clutched tightly in his hand, Joe is so busy trying to figure out 36 times 27 that he doesn't even notice Mr. Samson introduce Toby to Miss Phillips. He doesn't even hear Miss Phillips introduce Toby to the class.

Worst of all, he doesn't even hear Miss Phillips calling his name. "Joseph Rooney!" she repeats in her sharpest and squeakiest voice. "I asked you to stand up!"

Startled, Joe jumps to his feet, thinking he had been called on. "862!" he says loudly.

"Later, Joseph," Miss Phillips says, trying not to smile.

She turns to Toby. "You may take the empty seat directly behind Joseph. You'll get your books after recess."

"Thank you," Toby says politely, walking toward his new desk, looking at Joe's worried face, wondering if he should still try to be friends with him. Then he glances down and sees the sketch Joe had been working on when Miss Phillips had called on him.

He sees a drawing of a boy with a big head and a small body, and he reads the name Joe has printed across the bottom in big block letters: TOBY-SHMOBY!

At that moment, he wishes he were bigger and stronger than Joe, so he could hit him and knock him down and make him apologize. He wouldn't care if everyone watched. He wouldn't even care if Miss Phillips sent him to the principal.

"All right, Joseph," Miss Phillips says. "I believe you were about to tell us the answer to the first problem—36 times 27."

"Yes, ma'am," Joe answers confidently, pleased to be able to show Toby how smart he is. "36 times 27 equals 862."

"He's wrong, Miss Phillips!" Everyone turns to stare at Toby, who has hopped to his feet and raised his hand at the same time. "36 times 27 equals 972."

"Very good," says Miss Phillips. "But how did you do it so quickly?"

"I can do them all," Toby answers smugly. And before she can even have a chance to stop him, he rattles off every answer to every problem written on the blackboard without even taking a breath. "29 times 24 equals 696, 26 times 32 equals 832, 27 times 12 equals 324, 45 times 22 equals 990, 19 times 24 equals 456."

By the time he's finished, even Miss Phillips is staring

at him. After all, she's used to nine-year-old boys who throw spitballs or pass notes or whisper in class. But this is different. Why, even Miss Phillips couldn't do arithmetic problems so quickly in her head.

And that's only the beginning. When they get to history, Toby's hand is always up, correcting everybody's wrong answer. And when they get to geography, he even corrects Miss Phillips!

By the time they get to noon recess, Toby is feeling pretty proud of himself. Even when he sees Joe glaring at him, he doesn't care. He's shown everybody how smart he is, and he's sure that ought to count just as much as being able to ride a bicycle no-hands.

Poor Toby. He doesn't realize that being such a show-off is the best way to make yourself the most unpopular boy in the fourth grade.

Chapter Six:
Play ball!

Whap!

Joe drops his bat and races toward first base, as the ball sails far over the infield. On the sidelines, his classmates jump up and down in excitement.

"Attaboy, Joe!" yells Harry.

"It's a home run!" screams Mike.

"Home run! Home run!" shout the rest of the team as they watch Joe speed past first base and head for second.

The best part of the school day is recess. And the best part of recess is the softball game. And the best part of the softball game is always the time Joe Rooney comes to bat and hits another home run.

Joe may not know how much 36 times 27 is, but he is certainly the best baseball player in the fourth grade. Or even in the fifth grade, for that matter. And to his friends, that counts more than arithmetic or history or geography, or even being able to build a Geiger counter.

Joe rounds second base and heads for third, as an outfielder finally reaches the ball and throws it to the infield.

"Run, Joe, run!" his teammates scream.

"You can make it, Joe!" yells everybody in the fourth grade.

Well not quite everybody. One sad, lonely figure sits under a nearby tree, watching the softball game and wishing the kids would like him as much as they like Joe. But Toby has never hit a home run in his life. In fact, he has been so busy reading books and playing chess and being questioned by all those doctors that he has never even played baseball.

"Come on, Joe! Come on!" scream the kids as Joe rounds third base and charges toward home plate.

"Slide, Joe! Slide!" they yell as the second baseman gets the ball, whirls, and rifles it to the catcher.

"Home run! Home run!" they cry as the ball plops into the catcher's mitt, plops out again, and rolls away.

"You did it, Joe! You really did it!" they shout as Joe crosses home plate standing up and is immediately surrounded by all his teammates. It seems as if everybody in the fourth grade is gathered around Joe Rooney, slapping him on the back, congratulating him, and calling him a hero.

Well, not quite everybody. When the ball had plopped out of the catcher's mitt, it had rolled over to a tree under which a lonely boy sits, hit the tree trunk, and stopped. Toby doesn't even seem to notice the ball as he watches the kids around Joe and feels even more lonely than ever.

"Who's up next?" Joe asks.

"I am! I am!" Mike answers excitedly, waving the bat he is holding in his hand.

"Throw the ball, will you?" cries the catcher. He is looking toward Toby. "Come on. Throw it to me," he says, anxious to get the game started again.

Reluctantly, Toby gets to his feet, picks up the ball, and throws it. That is, he tries to throw it, but he's as bad at throwing a baseball as he is good at arithmetic and history and geography.

Joe, Harry, and Mike are all watching as the ball hits the ground at least ten feet away from where it was supposed to land, and the catcher has to go scrambling after it.

"Hey, look," Harry says. "The show-off can't throw a baseball!"

"I bet he doesn't even know how to play," Mike says.

"Yeah," Joe grins, suddenly thinking of a way to get even with Toby. "Time out!" he calls out to the team. Then he takes the bat from Mike and walks over to the tree, smiling his friendliest smile when he gets there.

Harry and Mike follow him, the way they always do.

"We need another man on our team," Joe says to Toby. "Want to play?"

"No," answers Toby, sure that Joe is just trying to trick him into something.

"Why? You scared?"

"I just don't want to play, that's all."

"I bet he doesn't know how," Mike says.

"What do you mean?" Joe says. "He knows everything." He smiles at Toby. "Don't you?"

"Leave me alone," Toby answers.

Joe shrugs. "I guess he's just a creep."

"I am not!" Toby retorts angrily.

"Then prove it," Joe challenges. He holds the bat out to Toby. "Here. You're up next."

Toby doesn't know what to do. He looks at the bat, and then he looks at the three boys staring at him, daring

him to get into the game. He looks at the bat again, wondering if he might be able to hit a home run, the way Joe had. That would show them, he thinks. That would teach them not to call him a creep.

Suddenly he makes up his mind, grabs the bat from Joe's hand, and walks toward home plate. The Phantoms of the Fourth Grade grin at each other as they scamper after him.

"At bat, Toby the Genius!" shouts Harry as he takes his place on the sidelines.

"Play ball!" yells Joe, grinning at his teammates.

Toby is so nervous when he steps up to the plate he is almost shaking. He takes a position, trying to remember how Joe had been standing when he hit that home run. But no matter how hard he tries to look as though he knows what he's doing, he looks just like a boy who has never played baseball in his life. His legs seem awkward, his hands are crossed over each other on the bat, and he wishes he had never let Joe dare him into trying to play.

But it's too late now. The pitcher winds up and throws the ball. Toby watches, squints, and swings. Plop! The ball hits into the catcher's mitt. Round and round spins Toby, falling to the ground in a cloud of dust.

"Strike one!" shouts Joe, grinning all the time.

"I could feel the breeze from here!" cries Harry.

Mike tries to yell something, but he is laughing so hard that his glasses fall off his nose. In fact, everyone in the fourth grade is laughing.

His face set in grim anger, Toby picks himself up from the ground and steps into the batter's box again. He'll still show them, he thinks. He's *got* to show them.

Again the pitcher throws the ball. Again Toby swings.

Again he misses. Again he spins around and around and falls to the ground.

"Strike two!" Even the team out in the field joins in the shout this time.

Laughter, giggles, shrieks, and whoops. Catcalls, taunting, shouting, roaring. Tears of anger in Toby's eyes. Cries of derision in his ears.

The whole fourth grade is on the sidelines now, all watching, yelling, chortling, waiting for him to spin around and fall to the ground.

Another pitch. Another swing. Another miss. Another spin. Another tumble to the ground.

Walls of laughter surround him. Screams of joy smother him. "Strike three! You're out!" they all cry.

No one laughs as hard as Joe does. That'll show him, he thinks. That'll teach him not to be such a show-off.

Slowly, Toby rises and looks around at the laughing faces. Most of all, he looks at Joe, and he thinks, I hate him. I wish he was dead. I wish he was dead.

He may very soon get that wish.

Chapter Seven:
Come on out, ghosts!

Toby is waiting.

The school day is over. The last bell has rung in the corridors and classrooms of Carlyle Elementary, and three hundred boys and girls are pouring out of the building. Through the schoolyard they move, talking, laughing, whispering, jumping, running, skipping, walking, hopping, shouting, whistling, singing.

All except Toby. For Toby is waiting.

Clutching his new books under his arm, he hides behind the biggest and broadest oak tree in the schoolyard. The sky is bright and blue, with only a few fleecy clouds to make it look even prettier. But Toby isn't interested in blue skies or fleecy clouds or even in the fun a kid can have after school on a beautiful October afternoon. He's interested in only one thing.

Getting even with Joe Rooney.

As he hides behind the oak tree and watches the kids go by, he remembers how it was in the classroom after recess. He remembers how the kids giggled at him every time he raised his hand to volunteer an answer. He remembers how they didn't care how smart he was or that he was almost a genius. All they cared about was how foolish he had looked in the softball game.

And it was all Joe Rooney's fault.

"Toby-Shmoby! Toby-Shmoby! Toby-Shmoby!" Now he hears the hated chant, and he knows Joe must be coming. Quickly, he presses even closer to the tree trunk. He wants to see Joe, but not now. Not until he can get him all alone.

The Phantoms of the Fourth Grade walk happily past the oak tree, singing their chant as they go. Joe, Harry, and Mike are on their way home from school, enjoying the blue skies, the fleecy clouds, and the beautiful October afternoon.

"Toby-Shmoby!" they sing as they race out of the school-yard, and they don't see the angry nine-year-old boy who steps away from the oak tree and watches them with narrowing eyes.

"Toby-Shmoby!" they chant as they chase each other down Market Street, and they don't notice the boy following them far down the block.

"Toby-Shmoby!" they chortle as they cut through an empty lot on Cherry Street and come out on a back road leading past Harper's Meadow. Down the elm-shaded road they trot, passing Mr. Todey's Auto Repair, cutting behind Mr. Capezio's junkyard, finally entering a narrow path through the brambles, rye grass, and weeds of an untended meadow.

Toby is not far behind.

Slowing down to a walk now, the three boys move along the deserted path in single file, with Joe in the lead, as always. There are no traffic noises in this lonely place, only the sound of tree frogs and occasional crickets, as they trudge along silently, their schoolbooks clutched under their arms.

The grass is so tall that Toby has difficulty keeping the boys in sight as he follows the path behind them. He wonders where they are going. Why are they taking this path? Is it a shortcut to their homes? Then he has a sudden and frightening thought that makes him stop and almost turn back.

Maybe they know I'm following them, he thinks. Maybe they're leading me into a trap so they can all jump on me at once.

By the time he decides to turn and follow them anyway, he finds he has no one to follow. The path up ahead is empty. The Phantoms of the Fourth Grade have disappeared!

No time to lose. Quickly, he races up the path, races between the brambles and the rye grass and the tall weeds, races until he reaches the top of a small rise in the overgrown meadow. And then he stops, ducking down in the high grass rippling in the October breeze.

Cautiously, he raises his head, parts the weeds blocking his view, and looks out into the meadow stretching below.

"Wow!" he says, his eyes widening in surprise at what he sees.

It isn't the small creek flowing down below that surprises Toby. Nor is it even the old wooden footbridge that crosses the creek. What makes his eyes widen is something standing in the meadow about fifty yards away from the rickety bridge.

That something is a house.

Not just an ordinary house, but a house with peeling paint and sagging doors and boarded-up windows and shingles flapping in the breeze. It's a real mess of a house, with weeds growing up to the creaking front door, with a broken ivy-trellis dangling down from the eaves, with birds flying out of the chimney, and with three small boys standing in the tall grass, staring up at the rusted rain gutters, and the broken shutters, and the most lonesome, sad, frightening excuse for a house that ever stood in a deserted meadow.

"I wonder whose house that is," Toby says to himself.

He wouldn't wonder if he had grown up in Carlyle, instead of having just moved here from New York. He would have known that the house has two names, one for the grownups, and one for the kids.

Grownups call it Harper House, because of old man Harper who once owned the house and the meadow, and who died more than twenty years ago without leaving any relatives behind to live in it.

Kids call it the Haunted House, because of the ghosts, and the goblins, and the bats, and the creaks, and the rattling chains, and all the other weird things kids know they'd find if they ever spent a night there.

Not that any kid has ever been brave enough to go to the Haunted House at night and try to find a ghost or a goblin. They're all much too scared for that. Even right now, in broad daylight, the deserted old house looks almost scary enough to frighten the bravest man on the Carlyle Police Force.

At least that's what the Phantoms of the Fourth Grade think as they stand about twenty feet away from the haunted house and look up at the boarded windows. Then Joe bends down and picks up a stone, as he always does when he comes here. So do Harry and Mike.

Joe looks at his friends and nods. Then they all look at

the house and shout. "Come on out, ghosts!" They yell. "Come on out!"

They throw the stones as hard as they can. Zap! Zap! Zap! Up against the side of the house, clattering down to the ground. The three friends turn and run. Why wait around and take chances, in case a real ghost does come out?

Toby stays in his hiding place, watching all this with great interest. He watches while the three boys stop running and turn and look at the house again. He listens while they shout once more.

"Come on out, ghosts! Come on out!"

He watches, and smiles to himself, and thinks how babyish these kids are to believe in things like ghosts and haunted houses. To Toby, that's almost as silly as believing in Santa Claus, or that toads can give you warts, or that stepping on an ant will make it rain, or that if you put a tooth under your pillow the Good Fairy will replace it with money.

Sometimes being almost a genius can make a boy miss half the fun of being nine years old.

Suddenly Toby stops smiling and raises himself a little higher in the tall grass. His three classmates seem to be finished throwing stones at the old house, and now he sees Harry and Mike saying goodbye to Joe. Toby edges forward a little as he watches Harry and Mike wandering off home through the meadow, while Joe turns in the opposite direction and walks slowly toward the old wooden bridge.

Toby's chance. Forgetting the path, he dashes forward through the weeds and brambles and rye grass, across the slope, down to the edge of the creek, reaching the bridge just before Joe is about to cross it.

Joe is so startled at Toby's unexpected appearance that he jumps, almost as if he had really seen a ghost this time.

He is even more startled when Toby stands in his way, not saying a word, just staring angrily at him.

Joe stares back at Toby.

Toby stares back at Joe.

Joe is determined to cross the bridge, even though Toby is standing directly in his path. He walks right up to the glowering boy and stops, waiting for Toby to get out of his way.

Toby doesn't move.

Neither does Joe.

Finally Toby takes a deep breath and says, "You're going to apologize."

"What for?"

"You made them laugh at me."

"I can't help it if you're a creep."

"You take that back!"

Joe smiles and chants, "Toby-Shmoby! Toby-Shmoby!"

"You take that back!" Toby cries again, dropping his books to the ground and jumping on Joe.

Taken by surprise, Joe falls to the damp ground at the edge of the creek, Toby on top of him. Over and over they roll, Toby hitting and kicking and doing everything he can to win the fight. But Joe is much bigger and stronger than Toby, and he gets to his feet without any trouble at all.

Toby jumps for him again, almost sobbing in his anger. Down goes Joe, losing his balance once more. He tries to get to his feet again, loses his balance again, and topples over into the stream.

Toby jumps up, races to the edge of the creek, fists clenched, ready for Joe when he climbs out of the water. But Joe isn't climbing anywhere.

Instead, he lies where he has fallen, eyes closed, head

sprawled on a sharp pointed rock, legs stretched out in the slowly moving water.

His eyes wide with fear, Toby stares at the still body. He panics. Breathing heavily, he scoops up his schoolbooks from the ground. Almost screaming, he turns and runs.

He runs through the meadow as fast as he can, through the brambles and the weeds and the waving high grass. He runs past Capezio's junkyard, past Mr. Todey's Auto Repair, down one street after another. He doesn't stop running until he is safe at home.

Joe's body still lies where he had fallen.

He doesn't move.

Chapter Eight:
Toby's fear

Murderer! Murderer! Murderer!

The words pound over and over again inside Toby's head as he sits at the dinner table with his mother and father. Everything tastes like prison food for him tonight. The honeydew melon, the roast beef and mashed potatoes, even the apple pie his mother has baked especially for him . . . all of them taste like bread and water.

Murderer! Murderer! Murderer!

He stands in his room and stares out at the dark mysterious night. All he can see is Joe Rooney, his eyes closed, lying where he has fallen. Joe Rooney, with his head on a rock and his legs floating in the creek.

Toby is frightened. More frightened than he has ever been in his life. He may be almost a genius, but he is also a nine-year-old boy, and he certainly doesn't want to spend the rest of his life in prison.

Behind him, the bedroom door opens slowly and Mr. Hammond enters the room. Any man who is bright enough to be promoted to head a new electronics plant is smart enough to know that something is bothering his son.

Mr. Hammond is also smart enough to know there are times a boy might want to keep his thoughts to himself. So he simply stands there, looks at his son, and says, "Hi, Toby."

"Hi," Toby answers, still looking out the window.

"How about a game of chess? Maybe I'll beat you tonight."

"No, thanks."

Toby still stares out the window. Mr. Hammond watches him, wishing there were some way he could get Toby to say what's bothering him.

Finally he takes a deep puff of the pipe he always seems to have in his mouth, and simply asks, "What's wrong, son?"

"Nothing," Toby shrugs. "Why?"

Mr. Hammond smiles. "Well, at dinner tonight, if I didn't know you were eating roast beef and mashed potatoes, I would have sworn you were eating bread and water."

Startled, Toby turns to stare at his father. How could any man be that smart? He had said exactly what Toby had been thinking. Could he know about Joe Rooney? Had the police called already?

"Come on, Toby," Mr. Hammond urges. "Something's bothering you. What is it?"

Toby takes a deep breath. "Dad, what happens to a kid who kills another kid. By accident, I mean."

"Well, I'm not a lawyer, but I imagine he might be sent to some kind of detention home. Why?"

"Just curious," Toby manages to answer. "We were talking about it at school."

"I see," says Mr. Hammond, not really seeing at all. He waits for Toby to say something more, but Toby can't think of anything to say except the truth, and he is much too frightened to say that. So, instead of saying anything, he turns and looks out the window once again.

"Well," sighs Mr. Hammond, "if you change your mind about the chess game, let me know."

"Okay, Dad," Toby answers, his eyes still fixed on the darkness outside.

He stands quiet and rigid, hoping his father won't ask any more questions. He doesn't move when he hears his father walk to the door, open it, and go out of the room.

He doesn't move when he hears the door close once again, even though it sounds to him like the clanging of a prison cell.

He doesn't even move when he thinks of how much his father and mother love him and how shocked they will be when the police come to arrest him for murder.

All he does is stare out the window.

And cry.

Chapter Nine: Please don't let him be dead

Morning.

The birds sing happily, the grass is wet with dew, and the sun shines down through a cloudless sky. It is a brisk October day, and the world should be a happy place.

But not for Toby. Breakfast is usually his favorite meal of all, but not today. Today the orange juice tastes like vinegar, the cereal like cardboard, the toast and jam like sour lemons, and the milk like house paint.

The doorbell hasn't chimed, and the phone hasn't rung, but Toby is still so worried that he feels as though a snake has crawled into his stomach and is chasing its tail around and around.

Maybe they don't like to arrest nine-year-old murderers at night, he thinks. Maybe they like to give them a good night's sleep before they drag them down to the police station, push them into a hard chair, shine a bright light at them, and put them through the third-degree.

Any minute now they'll come and take me away, he thinks, as he sits at the table and tries to eat one more bite of cardboard and sour lemons. They'll knock at the door and my parents will know what a monster I am, he thinks as he tries to drink one more sip of vinegar and house paint.

No knock. No chime. No telephone ring. But the snake still chases its tail as Toby sets out for school. Down Columbus Street he goes, feet dragging, wondering if the police will be waiting at the entrance to the schoolyard.

Suddenly, a happy thought. Maybe Joe isn't dead at all. Maybe he got up and went home and at this very moment is running around in the schoolyard playing ball with the rest of the fourth grade.

Toby grins a big wide grin as he starts to run toward school. The snake is gone from his stomach and the police are gone from his mind as he races as fast as his legs can move.

Face flushed, eyes bright, he rushes into the crowded schoolyard, rushes up to the mess of fourth grade kids playing in their usual corner, rushes up to find Harry and Mike and all the rest of them throwing a ball around. They are all there.

All but Joe.

Toby's eyes dart anxiously from side to side, hoping to see Joe off in some other corner of the schoolyard. All he sees are boys and girls of all sizes and shapes, tall and short, fat and thin, light and dark. He sees Miss Phillips looking at her watch, waiting for the bell to ring. He even sees Mr. Samson, the assistant principal, scowling at the noise as he crosses toward the school building.

What he doesn't see is Joe Rooney.

By the time the bell has rung and Miss Phillips has lined up the fourth grade, the snake has zupped down to Toby's stomach once again and is chasing its tail as madly as a squirrel in a cage.

"Did you see Joe Rooney?" Toby asks Harry anxiously as they stand in line.

"Why should I tell you?"

Toby turns to Mike. "Did you see Joe Rooney?" he asks again.

Mike shrugs. "Maybe his alarm didn't go off."

"All right, class! Follow me!" squeaks Miss Phillips as she starts toward the school building with the line straggling out behind her. "Eyes front!" she orders as she sees Toby trying to walk forward and look at the entrance to the schoolyard behind him, both at the same time. He looks and he looks, and he wishes and he wishes, but it doesn't do any good.

There is still no sign of Joe Rooney.

The school day unwinds slowly, like a big black snake stretching out in the hot summer sun. It is almost eleven o'clock, and Toby has given up all hope of seeing Joe rush in late with a note saying that he had overslept. Joe must really be dead, he thinks. In fact, he must still be lying with his legs in the creek and his head on the big hard rock.

"Please don't let him be dead," Toby whispers as he sits at his desk, unable to concentrate on the English composition Miss Phillips has assigned. "Please don't let him be dead," he prays as he stares at Joe's empty desk directly in front of him.

His composition paper is blank, but his troubled mind is filled with frightening pictures. He sees a cemetery, and an open grave, and a coffin. He sees Harry and Mike and all the rest of Joe's friends, all dressed in funeral black, all staring at him accusingly.

What he doesn't see is Miss Phillips come up alongside his desk and squinting as she looks down at his blank paper. "Is something wrong, Toby?" she asks.

Toby is so startled he almost yells. And when Miss Phillips starts to ask him why he isn't writing his composition, he suddenly jumps up from his desk and rushes out of the room!

"Toby! Toby!" Miss Phillips shouts as everyone in the class turns to see what is going on.

"Toby! Toby!" she calls as she rushes to the classroom door to see the frightened boy racing madly down the corridor.

Out into the schoolyard he runs, heart pounding, legs churning, hair flying in the wind. Past the big oak tree he rushes, through the open gate, down the sun drenched street. Faster and faster he goes, across the empty lot on Cherry Street, out into the back road leading past Harper's Meadow.

Only one thought is in his mind as he races past Mr. Todey's Auto Repair, cuts behind Mr. Capezio's junkyard, stumbles into the narrow path through the brambles, rye grass, and tall weeds of the untended meadow. He must find Joe, he sobs to himself. He must find Joe and pull him out of the creek where he had fallen.

Gasping for breath, he staggers along the path, tumbling into a bramble, picking himself up, and moving on. The deserted house is not far ahead, and near it is the creek, and in the creek he knows he will find the dead body of Joe Rooney.

He reaches the rise, stares for a moment at the lonely old house, then rushes down to the rickety bridge and the slowly moving creek.

The water moves sluggishly along. The rocks glisten in the October sun. The old bridge creaks in the breeze. And that is all.

There is no sign of Joe Rooney. He is gone.

Chapter Ten:
Into the dark room

Gone. Joe's body is gone.

Someone must have found him, Toby thinks as he stares down at the spot where Joe had fallen. Someone must have found him and taken him home.

He starts running again. Across the creaking bridge, down through another path, out into Parmalee Road. Along the road he rushes, past the frame houses and their gardens, past the mailboxes standing like frozen sentinels along the side, looking, always looking.

HepworthMarshallTracyAronJonesSimpson. The names on the mailboxes whiz by as Toby races past each one, hoping that Joe lives on this street. CrowellAdamsWestConradRoss-RooneyTaylor. Rooney! The name on that mailbox was Rooney!

A few steps more and Toby is leaning against the white mailbox, breathing heavily, looking at the small neat house in front of which it stands. He looks at the porch, at the freshly painted front door, at the lace curtains framing the windows, at the weathered gray shingles covering the sloping roof.

He looks at all these things, but in his mind he sees a dead boy lying with his legs in a creek and his head on a sharp rock. For a moment he thinks maybe he should run away. Only for a moment. Instead, he catches his breath and walks slowly up to the house, climbs the two steps onto the porch, and peers in through one of the lace-covered windows.

He sees an ordinary living room filled with ordinary living room furniture. What he doesn't see is the elderly, sad-faced, gray-haired man who comes up on the porch behind him, and stands quietly watching Toby peering through the window.

"What do you want, boy?" the old man finally growls.

Toby turns sharply, so startled he can't even speak.

"Looking for something?" the old man asks.

"I came about Joe," Toby manages to say.

"Shouldn't you be in school, boy?"

"I have to know about him," Toby says anxiously.

The old man's shoulders are bent with age, his huge hands are calloused and worn, but his eyes are bright and piercing. They stare at Toby as if they can read everything that is going on in his mind.

"Come on inside," he finally says, and shuffles slowly to the front door and holds it open. Toby doesn't move. He has come this far, but he doesn't know if he is brave enough to go into the house. "Come on in, boy," the old man says impatiently. "I won't bite you."

Toby can do one of two things. He can either run away,

or he can go into the house. The only thing he can't do is stand there forever and look at the old man holding the front door open.

He goes into the house.

The old man follows, closing the door behind him. "I'm Joe's grandfather," he says. He studies Toby with his piercing eyes. "Guess you know what happened to him."

"It was an accident," Toby says quickly, feeling sure Joe's grandfather knows who was responsible.

The old man points to a closed bedroom door. "He's in there. Want to see him?"

"No, sir," Toby replies, shaking his head vigorously.

"If you're a friend of his, you'll want to see him. Come on." And without giving Toby a chance to protest, Joe's grandfather shuffles to the closed door and pulls it open.

Toby can't see much from where he stands, but he does see a dark room with the shades drawn, and the last thing in this world he wants to do is walk into the dark room and see whatever there is to see.

The old man scowls at Toby. "Go on in, boy," he says. "You came this far. Go on in."

Toby's feet are made of lead, and that snake is running around and around in his stomach as he forces himself to move to the threshold of that dark, gloomy room that seems to smell of death. He can see the bed now. Not only that, but he can see the still body of a nine-year-old boy lying on that bed. It's too dark to see much more, but Toby knows just what he would see if Joe's grandfather ever were to pull up the shade.

He knows he would see Joe Rooney's dead body, lying still, waiting for the funeral.

He almost screams aloud as Joe's grandfather crosses to the window and starts to raise the shade. Trembling with fear, he closes his eyes tightly and wonders if he will ever be able to open them again.

The shade goes up. Daylight floods the small room. Toby can feel the brightness pressing against his eyelids. He is so frightened, he can hardly breathe.

Slowly, he opens his eyes and looks at the bed.

Chapter Eleven:
A rainfall
of giggles

"Who is it?" a sleepy voice asks.

The voice comes from Joe Rooney, lying on the bed, his face pale, a big white bandage wrapped around his head, his eyes fluttering open as the sunlight awakens him.

"He's all right!" shouts Toby as the whirling snake in his stomach dissolves into pure sweet happiness. "He's all right!" he cries again, almost unable to keep from dancing with joy.

"Of course he's all right," says Joe's grandfather. "A bump on the head, and a sprained ankle to keep him out of school a couple of weeks. Maybe next time he won't try to jump across that creek." He smiles fondly at Joe, then glances at Toby. "Want some milk and cookies, boy?"

"No, thank you." Toby still can't believe his eyes. Joe is alive! Really alive!

"Can't stay too long," Joe's grandfather says as he goes out of the room, leaving the two boys alone.

Toby and Joe look at each other silently for a moment. It isn't easy for two boys to have a conversation when the last time they had seen each other, they had been rolling over and over and fighting near the creek.

"Hi," Toby finally says as he slowly approaches the bed.

"Hi," Joe answers, watching Toby moving toward him. "What are you doing here, anyway?"

"I was worried about you."

"Oh."

"You really going to be out of school for two weeks?"

"That's what the doctor said." Joe touches his bandage proudly. "I've got six stitches in my head."

"Wow!"

Specks of dust dance in the sunlight. The window curtain stirs slightly in the breeze. Photographs of baseball stars look down from the walls. Toby and Joe look at each other, each wondering what to say next.

"You didn't tell them I did it," Toby finally says.

"Think I'm a fink?" Joe glares at Toby. "Anyway, you were just lucky. I could've beat you easy."

Toby glares back at Joe. "You shouldn't have called me a creep."

"You shouldn't be such a show-off."

"If I'm a show-off, so are you."

"I am not!"

"Yes, you are," Toby says. "The day I moved in. Riding no-hands past my house. That was showing off."

"That was different."

"Why?"

"Because that was bicycles, not schoolwork."

"It's still showing off."

"It's not the same."

"You're just sore, 'cause I'm smarter than you are."

"You're just sore, 'cause you can't play baseball or ride a bike no-hands or anything."

Joe lies on the bed, staring at Toby. Toby stands in the room, glaring at Joe. They glare and they glare, each boy determined not to look away or flinch or blink his eyes.

A glaring contest can sometimes be just as important as a fistfight.

The only trouble is that staring straight into someone's eyes for a long time can make you want to giggle. Toby bites his lips. So does Joe. Toby feels a giggle starting in the back of his throat. So does Joe. Toby tries hard to fight it back, wanting to look fierce and angry. So does Joe.

Sometimes it's easier to fight a hurricane or an avalanche than a giggle that's determined to come out. First, the corners of your mouth turn up. You force them down, but they turn up again anyway. Then, your cheeks puff up as the giggles press hard against your teeth, and your whole face shakes as you try to keep them inside. Then, before you can stop them, they come pouring out, pattering in the room like raindrops in a puddle.

The boys giggle and giggle, and then giggle some more, until Joe's head begins to hurt. They try to stop and can't, because giggles have a life of their own. And before they are through, the two boys who had been glaring at each other are laughing so hard that they have forgotten what they were angry about.

"How come you're not in school?" Joe finally manages to ask.

"I ran out," Toby replies, still giggling a little.

"Really?"

"Uh-huh. I ran right out of the classroom."

"How come?"

"Because I wanted to."

"Gosh!" Joe exclaims, staring at Toby with admiration. "What did old lady Phillips do?"

"She yelled," Toby says, grinning at Joe.

"Really? What'd she say?"

" 'Toby! Toby!' Just like that," Toby says, imitating Miss Phillips' squint and squeaky voice so perfectly that Joe starts laughing all over again. " 'Toby! Toby!' " he repeats.

"Toby! Toby! Toby!" they both shout, trying to laugh and giggle and talk all at the same time. They are laughing so hard that they don't notice Joe's grandfather enter the room and stand there watching them, a gentle smile on his lips.

"All right, boy," he finally says to Toby. "Time to go."

"Aw, Grandpa," Joe protests. "Does he have to?"

"He can come another time."

"I better get back to school anyway," Toby says, "or I'll be in real trouble." He glances toward the bed and grins. "See you later, Joe."

"See you."

"Goodbye, Mr. Rooney," Toby says to Joe's grandfather. Then, waving goodbye to Joe once again, he hurries out of the house and down the road back toward school.

He is smiling.

In the room of the house on Parmalee Road, Joe leans his bandaged head back on his pillow, stares up at the ceiling, and thinks about Toby.

He is smiling, too.

Chapter Twelve:
We'll show 'em!

Mr. Samson removes his glasses and polishes them with his tie. He sighs deeply, wishing he were somewhere fishing, instead of sitting in his office with a frightened boy who has been sent down from Miss Phillips' class. The only thing is, Toby doesn't seem to be frightened. In fact, Mr. Samson would almost swear he sees a smile on Toby's lips.

"In this school, young man, we do not allow students to jump up and run out of class whenever they like," says the assistant principal, trying to scowl at Toby.

"I'm sorry, sir," says Toby, smiling to himself as he remembers the way he and Joe had giggled together.

"Do you find this funny, young man?" demands Mr. Samson sharply. He puts his glasses back on and stares at Toby through their thick lenses.

"Oh no, sir," says Toby, almost giggling out loud when he remembers how scared he had been that Joe was dead.

"Then I would like an explanation, if you don't mind." Mr. Samson is puzzled. Nine-year-old boys aren't usually happy when they are sent down to his office. He watches Toby carefully. "I want the truth," he adds.

"Joe Rooney was absent," says Toby, "and I was afraid something had happened to him." And that, of course, is the truth. Part of it, anyway.

"He must be a very good friend of yours."

"Oh yes, sir," says Toby proudly. "He's the best friend I have in the whole school." This time he doesn't even try to hide the grin that stretches from one side of his face to the other, a grin that seems to say, "Look at me! I have a friend! A real friend!"

It is such a beautiful grin that even Mr. Samson finds himself smiling while he warns Toby not to let it happen again.

The grin is still there when Toby rushes home from school, races to his room, snatches some books from his shelves, dumps his chess set in a box, and darts out again.

The grin is the first thing Joe's grandfather sees when he opens the front door, says hello to Toby, and watches him hurry into Joe's room.

The grin is on Joe's face, too, when he sees the adventure books Toby has brought him and watches Toby unpack his chess set.

"I don't know how to play chess," says Joe.

"I'll teach you," smiles Toby.

That is the beginning. Every day after that, Toby can hardly wait to get home from school. Suddenly it doesn't seem to matter that none of the other kids like him.

"I have a friend," he says to himself each day as he throws his books down in his room and hurries out to Joe's house, bringing books and games and anything else that might make Joe's days pass more quickly.

Toby teaches Joe how to play chess, showing him the moves and the special tricks, laughing together over Joe's mistakes, rejoicing together when Joe almost manages to win a game.

Joe teaches Toby how to play baseball, showing him how to hold a bat, how to stand, giggling together over Toby's clumsiness, shout with joy when Toby swings the bat in the room and hits an imaginary home run.

"I have an idea," says Toby. "We'll spend half the time playing chess and the other half practicing baseball. Okay?"

"Okay."

The days go by. Joe improves, his wound heals, and he is able to hobble outside for baseball practice.

Nobody ever saw baseball practice like this! The pitcher is leaning on a crutch in his back yard. The batter stands in front of an elm tree, eyes narrowed, concentrating with all his might. The pitcher throws the ball, almost falling down. The batter swings, misses, and *does* fall down!

They don't know which part of the afternoon is more fun. One day, they'll think it's the chess game, when Toby is the teacher, and another day they'll laugh more when it's baseball practice and Joe is the teacher.

"Maybe you ought to borrow my crutch!" Joe would shout as Toby misses the ball and falls to the ground.

"Maybe you ought to borrow my head!" Toby would shout as he wins a chess game in six moves, and Joe crosses his eyes in despair.

Sometimes the most fun is when they're just sitting and talking. Toby tells Joe about the noise and the traffic and the tall buildings of New York City, and Joe tells Toby about the swimming hole and riding a bike through Mr. Cooper's leaf pile and the haunted house in Harper's Meadow.

But the greatest day of all, the most wonderful, mar-

velous, sunshiny, joyous, unbelievable day in the world is the day when Joe pitches, Toby swings, connects, and the ball goes sailing far over Joe's head!

"Home run! That'd be a home run!" Joe shouts.

"I did it! I really did it!" Toby screams, dancing up and down, crossing his eyes, grinning his grin, throwing his bat high in the air, and whooping and hollering so loudly that Joe's grandfather comes running out to see if the world is coming to an end.

It isn't. In fact, the world is alive and well and bright. And it gets brighter and brighter every time Toby connects with one of Joe's pitches and thinks of how surprised the kids in school are going to be.

"Toby Hammond, the Home Run King!" cries Joe.

"We'll show 'em!" shouts Toby. "We'll really show 'em!"

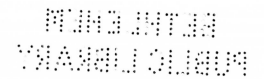

Chapter Thirteen:
Nothing changes

Toby leans against the schoolyard fence, books under his arm, smiling his secret smile. Surrounded by the early morning noise and bedlam, he stands by himself, as usual. But this time he doesn't care.

Harry Kurawicz, Mike Rizzo, and all the other fourth grade kids can throw a ball around all they like. They can ignore him while they run and jump and sing and play, the way they always do. They can whisper about him, say nasty things about him, or even call him names, but he doesn't care.

Not any more. Not when the most popular boy in the whole fourth grade is his very best friend. It was a secret up to now, but soon all the other kids will know it, too. They'll know it because Joe Rooney's bandage and crutch are gone, he doesn't even limp, and he's coming back to school this morning.

Toby can't wait to hear what the other kids will say when they see him and Joe together. More than that, he can hardly wait for the softball game and the home run he is sure he will hit.

So he leans against the fence, smiles his secret smile, and dreams a dream that will never happen.

It is almost time for the first bell. Miss Phillips looks at her watch and sighs. Mr. Samson crosses through the schoolyard and groans. The kids toss their ball around and shout. Toby glances toward the entrance gate and grins.

He's here. Joe is just entering and looks as good as new. Dodging through the schoolyard, almost tripping over his own feet, Toby rushes excitedly up to his new friend.

"Hi, Joe," he says.

"Hi, Toby," Joe grins back.

"How're you feeling?"

"Okay."

"Listen, Joe. Do you want to play chess after school today?"

Toby never gets the answer to that question, for by that time Harry and Mike have seen Joe and come rushing over to him, followed by all the other kids in the fourth grade.

"Hey, Joe!" yells Harry.

"How are you, Joe?" shouts Mike.

"How's your leg?" screams Sam Plover.

"You going to be able to play ball?" asks someone else.

They all surround Joe, all talking at once, happy to see him, yelling, laughing, chattering, pulling him along with them, as Joe laughs back, glad to see all his friends again. He's still the most popular kid in the class, as he always was.

And Toby is left standing all by himself, as he always was.

Nothing changes.

Chapter Fourteen:
Take my turn at bat

Toby can't believe it. He refuses to believe it. He's sure Joe didn't mean to walk off and leave him standing alone, just like that. After all, Joe hadn't seen his other friends for two weeks, and they had a lot to talk about.

Toby is sure it will be different at noon recess when Joe has a chance to talk to him, and all the kids will see how friendly they are.

That's what Toby is thinking as he sits at his desk, writing a note, while Miss Phillips puts a spelling exercise on the blackboard. He leans forward, taps Joe on the shoulder, and quickly hands him the slip of paper he had torn from his notebook, hoping Miss Phillips hasn't seen him.

The teacher is much too busy at the blackboard to imagine her best student passing a note, but Harry Kurawicz isn't doing anything at all, and he sits at the desk next to Joe.

Harry leans over as Joe unfolds the piece of paper and reads what Toby has written. He looks over Joe's shoulder and almost giggles out loud when he sees the question Toby is asking Joe.

"Do you want to play chess after school?" the note says.

Chess? Does the class creep really expect Joe to play with him? And a real creepy game like chess? That's what Harry thinks when he points back and forth from Joe to Toby and almost giggles again.

Joe looks at the note, and then he looks at Harry. Harry grins, a grin that seems to say, "Imagine the nerve of that creep! Imagine him thinking you'd want to be friends with him!"

Now Joe could do many things. He could tell Harry to mind his own business. Or he could tell Harry that Toby wasn't really as bad as all the other kids thought he was. Or he could even tell Harry that he has been playing chess with Toby every day for the past two weeks.

He could do any of those things. But with Harry sitting there and grinning and watching him, Joe is ashamed to admit that he and Toby have become friends.

Instead, he picks up his pencil, prints a great big "NO" on Toby's note, and hands it back. Then he grins at Harry, as if to say, "You're right. Only a creep would want to be friends with a creep."

Toby looks at the answer on his note, looks at Joe and Harry smiling at each other, and his lips tighten in anger. They're still against me, he thinks. Everybody in this school is against me.

Toby is still angry at noon recess, when he sits in his usual lonely place under the usual tree, watching the usual softball game. It's almost Joe's turn at bat, but Toby doesn't care. He doesn't care about anything, now that he knows friendship can't even be trusted.

What he doesn't know is that Joe feels just as terrible as he does. "I'm a traitor and a coward," Joe thinks as he holds the bat in his strong hands. "Toby is my friend, and I shouldn't be ashamed to say so, no matter what the fellers think."

He looks at Toby sitting under the tree, thinks about the chess games and the baseball practice, remembers the giggles and laughter, and suddenly decides to tell him he's sorry for what he did.

It's easy to decide, but not so easy to do. When Joe walks over to Toby and opens his mouth to apologize, all that comes out is, "Hi." Toby just stares at him without answering, then looks down at the ground between his feet.

"You mad?" Joe asks.

"I thought we were friends," Toby replies, still staring at the ground.

"Sure we are."

"You don't act like it."

"Here," Joe says suddenly, holding the bat out to Toby. "Take my turn at bat."

"Why should I?"

"So we can show them you're not a creep."

Toby looks at the bat. Then he looks at Joe's anxious face. Then he looks at the bat again. But what he sees is something else.

What he sees is the pitcher winding up. He sees himself in the batter's box, confident, poised, waiting for the ball. He sees the pitch come. Whap! He races around the bases as the ball sails further than any ball that was ever hit in the history of the world. He sees himself crossing home plate surrounded by the yelling and screaming and cheering of every kid who ever went to Carlyle Elementary School. Up on their shoulders he is lifted, and paraded around the schoolyard like a conquering hero!

That's what he sees. What he hears is Harry Kurawicz yelling. "Come on, Joe!" Harry calls. "You're up!"

"You can do it, Toby," Joe says. "Just remember what I taught you."

Suddenly Toby jumps to his feet, grins, and grabs the bat. "Okay," he says. "I'll show them."

He hurries toward home plate.

Chapter Fifteen:
The return
of Toby-Shmoby

It doesn't take long for word to get around the school-yard that Toby Hammond is at bat instead of Joe. It takes even less time for the fourth grade kids to come running to the sidelines to laugh and giggle and shout.

Toby stands nervously in the batter's box, trying to re-member everything Joe had taught him. He places his feet carefully, holds the bat with a firm grip, and tries his best not to hear the shouts that surround him.

"Toby-Shmoby, the home run king!" cries Harry.

"Don't fall on your face, Toby-Shmoby!" yells Mike.

Joe stands next to the other two Phantoms of the Fourth Grade, but he isn't laughing and he isn't shouting. What he wants most of all is for Toby not to look silly. Then he won't be ashamed to show that he's his friend.

The pitcher throws the ball. More anxious than he has ever been in his life, Toby swings. He misses. Not only does he miss, but he whirls around and around and falls to the ground, just as he had done before.

Roars of laughter fill his ears as he lies in the dirt. Shouts and screeches and yells pound him as he gets angrily to his feet. And then, worst of all, he hears the hated chant begin.

"Toby-Shmoby! Toby-Shmoby! Toby-Shmoby!"

Started by Harry, echoed by Mike, it spreads to all the fourth graders. "Toby-Shmoby!" they all sing. "Toby-Shmoby! Toby-Shmoby!"

All but Joe. Disgusted, almost as nervous as Toby, Joe prays for his friend to hit the next pitch, and motions for him to grip the bat more tightly. But Toby doesn't notice. In fact, he doesn't notice anything but the chant in his ears and the laughing faces and the pitcher winding up and throwing the ball.

He swings again. He misses again. He falls on his face again.

"TOBY-SHMOBY! TOBY-SHMOBY! TOBY-SHMOBY!"

The chant is endless, like the swinging of a pendulum that will never stop. Even Joe can't help grinning at how funny Toby looks when he sprawls to the ground.

Up on his feet, his face red with anger and embarrassment. How could this happen? he wonders. I was going to be a hero. I was going to show them all.

Into the batter's box again, standing awkwardly, forgetting everything Joe had ever taught him. He looks worried, silly, frightened, desperate, almost about to burst into tears.

"TOBY-SHMOBY! TOBY-SHMOBY! TOBY-SHMOBY!"

It rises from the sidelines like mist from a meadow, covering everything around it. Harry is chanting. Mike is chanting. Sam Plover is chanting. Everyone is chanting. Everyone but Joe.

"Come on, Joe!" shouts Harry. "You made up the name!"

"Yeah," says Joe, feeling embarrassed for Toby but not wanting the other kids to notice.

"Then come on!" insists Harry. "Toby-Shmoby! Toby-Shmoby! Toby-Shmoby!"

"Toby-Shmoby!" Joe chants finally, not wanting to seem different from the other kids. "Toby-Shmoby! Toby-Shmoby! Toby-Shmoby!" he sings, wishing he were brave enough to tell them to stop.

The last pitch. The last swing. Around and around and down to the ground, with even the bat flying out of Toby's hand!

"TOBY-SHMOBY! TOBY-SHMOBY! TOBY-SHMOBY!"

Up to the batter's box they rush, surrounding the unhappy boy sprawled on the ground, their mouths open wide, their mocking chant so loud that even the buildings seem to shake.

And Joe is now chanting as loudly as the rest.

"TOBY-SHMOBY! TOBY-SHMOBY! TOBY-SHMOBY!"

Up to his feet, face flushed, eyes glistening with tears of anger, Toby stares directly into the face of the boy he had thought was his best friend.

"TOBY-SHMOBY! TOBY-SHMOBY! TOBY-SHMOBY!" shouts Joe with the rest of the fourth graders.

Even Joe! Even the boy who had read his books and played chess with him and taught him how to hit a base-ball! "I hate you!" Toby wants to scream! "I hate all of you," he wants to shriek. He wants to roar, but his mouth won't open. He wants to shout, but words won't come.

He runs. Across the schoolyard, into the building, any-where he can be alone and cry and wish they were all dead.

Chapter Sixteen:
The scream

Revenge.

Nothing else is in Toby's mind. Not baseball nor chess or books or teachers or doctors with long beards and thick spectacles. Only Joe Rooney. Only the way Joe had laughed with the rest of the kids, had called him names, had been a worse traitor than Benedict Arnold. Well, Benedict Arnold had been shot for betraying his country.

Now it will be Joe Rooney's turn.

They all think they're better than I am, Toby thinks angrily. Just because they can play baseball and ride a bike no-hands and stupid things like that. And I'm just as stupid for trying to learn to play baseball just so they would like me.

They don't have to like me, Toby thinks. I'm smarter than they are, and that's all that matters. And before I'm through, they'll really know how smart I am!

That afternoon, there isn't a question or a problem that Toby doesn't answer. His arm keeps shooting up like a rocket almost before anyone else in the class can open his mouth, until even Miss Phillips has to tell him to give some-one else a chance.

But Toby doesn't care. The only thing that matters now is showing them that his brains are more important than their baseball game. How many of them can read a book on philosophy? How many of them can build a Geiger counter? How many of them can even do long division? By the time the last bell rings there isn't a kid in the class who doesn't know who is the smartest nine-year-old they had ever seen.

But it still isn't enough.

I've got to find some way to get even with Joe, Toby thinks as he walks through the schoolyard all by himself.

I've got to teach Joe not to be a traitor, he thinks as he wanders down the street without noticing where he's going.

I've got to show Joe what it's like to be laughed at, he thinks as he walks through a path surrounded by rye grass and brambles and weeds. And before he even realizes it, he is standing beside a creek near a rickety bridge, looking down at the very spot where Joe had once fallen and hit his head.

He sits on a tree stump and thinks about many things. He thinks about his apartment in New York City, about kids, loneliness, laughter, tears, bicycles, Geiger counters, moving men, bearded doctors, about all the whys and wherefores that make a nine-year-old boy perch on a stump in a deserted meadow and dream about revenge.

Revenge. There must be a way. His gaze wanders over toward the old decaying house standing not more than fifty yards away. He stares at the boarded-up windows, the creaky shutters, the peeling paint, the flapping shingles.

He stares and stares and feels the beginning of an idea tingle in his brain.

The tingle becomes a buzz, the buzz becomes a roar, and Toby suddenly jumps to his feet and starts running. He doesn't stop until he reaches his house, races through the living room, charges into his bedroom, and flings his closet door open.

Down comes a suitcase. Into the suitcase goes the portable tape recorder his father had bought him for his ninth birthday. A Boy Scout knife. From the cellar, a hammer and a saw and a pair of scissors. From the garage, a length of good stout rope. The suitcase is snapped shut, and Toby is on his way.

The old house looks down at the deserted meadow. The small boy carries the loaded suitcase through the tall weeds, coming closer and closer, until he is almost at the creaking, cracking, weathered front door.

Standing with the suitcase in his hand, Toby looks warily at the entrance to the old house all the kids think is haunted. He has come this far, but now he is nervous. There is no one here but him and the house, no sound but the rustle of the wind in the meadow.

In the nearby creek, a bullfrog croaks. On the rooftop, a jet black crow waits. In the meadow, a snake slithers through the grass. If there were such things as ghosts, this is just where they would live. This is where they would rattle their chains and howl and moan and make your hair stand on end until it turns white with terror.

Toby gulps. He leans against the door and pushes.

C-R-E-A-K!

The weathered old door slowly swings inward on its hinges. A dim light filters in through the dark and dusty interior for the first time in many years. Slowly, cautiously, always ready to run, Toby steps over the threshold and into the musty, cobwebbed, littered, echoing, smelly old living room.

He looks around, trying to keep from trembling. He sees an old fireplace covered with dust. He sees a few pieces of broken-down furniture surrounded by shattered chairs and tables and piles of crates and cartons. He sees a stairway leading up to the second floor with cobwebs hanging from the banister. He sees torn papers and broken bottles and scattered remnants of a long-dead past.

The rising breeze whistles through the boards covering the windows, as Toby nervously approaches a shaky old table and sets his suitcase on its dusty surface. With shaky but determined fingers he starts to undo the catch.

Suddenly, a noise! A flutter of wings, and something zips down the chimney and into the room! Toby jumps, almost knocking the suitcase to the floor. He whirls, sees the something fluttering wildly around and around in the dimness! He runs for the door, and the something rushes past him and out into the sunlight.

A bird. It is only a bird, but Toby is still trembling as he clings to the half-opened door. He wants to run away, and leave this old house behind him. He wants to dash into the sunlight like the bird and escape from the cobwebs and the dark shadows.

But he wants more than that. He also wants revenge against Joe Rooney and his friends. He wants to laugh at them, as they had laughed at him. So he doesn't run at all.

Instead, he slowly closes the door and slips the bolt shut. The outside is gone. Nothing is here but Toby and the nameless fears lurking in the corners.

There are no ghosts, he says to himself as he crosses to his suitcase. "There are no ghosts," he repeats aloud as he undoes the latch and pulls out his tape recorder.

He stands quietly for a moment, trying not to be frightened. He looks at the tape recorder and plugs in the microphone. He switches on the current, puts the microphone to his mouth. He takes a deep breath.

He screams!

Chapter Seventeen:
The challenge

"I'll bet you won't," says Harry.

"I bet I will," says Toby.

The two boys stand facing each other in the school-yard, only a short distance away from where Joe is setting up today's softball game. Mike stands beside them, polishing his glasses as he looks at Toby in amazement.

"You will not," says Mike.

"I will so," says Toby.

"I bet you'll be too scared," says Harry.

"I bet I won't," says Toby.

"Hey, Joe!" Harry suddenly calls out. "Come on over here!"

Joe walks slowly toward the three boys. He hasn't talked to Toby since yesterday, because he can't really think of what to say. He knows he should apologize for calling Toby names along with the rest of the kids, but "I'm sorry" are sometimes the hardest words in the world to pronounce.

It's much easier for Joe to tell himself that Toby did look a creep yesterday. More than that, he sure acted like a creep when ke kept showing off in class all afternoon after the ball game. In fact, any kid who thinks being smart in school is more important than knowing how to play baseball or ride a bike no-hands or climb a tree deserves to be called a creep.

That's what Joe keeps telling himself as he walks over to Toby and Harry and Mike. People can be funny sometimes. Even when they're wrong, they spend so much time thinking up reasons why they're right that they never have time to say, "I'm sorry."

Mike looks at Joe. "Know what Toby-Shmoby says?"

"What?"

"He says he's gonna go to the haunted house after dark tonight, and he's gonna stay there until midnight."

Joe stares at Toby. "What about the ghosts?"

"There's no such thing."

"You wanna bet?" asks Mike.

"Only creeps believe in ghosts," Toby says to Joe.

"You wanna bet?" asks Mike for the second time.

"Well, I'm not scared," Toby says firmly, "and I dare you to go with me." He looks directly at Joe. "I double dare you."

Toby can hardly keep from smiling as he watches the Phantoms of the Fourth Grade looking worriedly at each other. He knows they can't turn down a dare, so he knows the first part of his scheme is working perfectly.

"What time are you going?" Joe finally asks.

"Ten o'clock," Toby answers promptly.

"But I have to be in bed by nine-thirty," Mike complains.

"So do I," Harry says quickly, anxious to find some way to get out of it.

"Me, too," agrees Joe, hoping Toby will change his mind.

"That makes it easier," says Toby, who has thought of

everything. "Your parents will think you're still in bed. All you have to do is sneak out of your room after your door is closed. Go out the window and meet me at the haunted house."

"But my bedroom's on the second floor. I can't sneak out," Mike complains, forgetting how many times he has climbed down the drainpipe.

"You just want to get out of it," Toby accuses. "You're chicken."

"I am not!"

"Then you'll meet me?"

"You bet I will!"

"How about you?" Toby is looking at Harry and Joe.

"We'll be there," says Joe, wishing he had never met Toby.

"We sure will," adds Harry, wishing Toby had never moved to Carlyle.

Toby smiles broadly. "Okay, then," he says. "Ten o'clock. At the haunted house."

Chapter Eighteen:
Into the
haunted house

Somewhere a dog howls. From somewhere else a bull-frog croaks. Overhead, dark scudding clouds cover the stars and the tiny sliver of a moon. A low moaning wind moves through the deserted meadow, touching the brambles and the rye grass and tall, tall weeds.

The big old lonely house sits in the darkness like a scarred and battered ogre, its eyes boarded up, its skin cracked and peeling, its stomach rumbling and creaking with each gust of wind. Above it circle the nighthawks, gliding on motionless wings. At its feet stand two small figures, trembling at the blackness around them.

Harry and Mike have been the first to arrive. And now they wait, each with his flashlight, each wishing he were home in bed, each determined not to let the other know how frightened he is.

"It sure is dark," Harry says, trying to keep his teeth from chattering.

"It sure is," Mike agrees, trying to keep his knees from knocking.

"You scared?"

"Nah. Are you?"

"Nah."

A rustle in the grass behind them!

"What's that?" gasps Mike, praying it isn't a ghost.

"I don't know," moans Harry, hoping he doesn't faint.

"Shine your flashlight!" cries Mike as they whirl toward the menacing rustle behind them.

Two beams of light shine in the darkness. Two beams of light cut twin paths through the dark and fearful night. Two beams of light punch holes through the rising mist, revealing a figure moving toward them.

"Turn the lights away!" cries Joe Rooney as he approaches. "They're shining right in my eyes!"

"Whew," sighs Mike, pointing his flashlight down to the ground.

"Mike thought you were a ghost," says Harry, trying to sound brave.

"Harry thought you were a monster," says Mike, trying to sound even braver.

"Where's Toby?" Joe asks, looking around at the darkness.

"I don't know," Harry answers.

Joe glances up at the dark deserted house looming above them like a giant silent toad waiting to gobble up three small boys. "It sure looks scary," he whispers.

"Yeah," agrees Mike, feeling his knees start to knock again. "I bet Toby changed his mind."

"I bet he did," offers Harry eagerly. "No use waiting around here for him."

"That's right," Mike says quickly. "Let's not stay here. Let's go home."

"What if he comes?" asks Joe, still looking nervously at the empty old house.

"He won't come," says Harry. "He's too chicken."

"Harry's right," says Mike, turning anxiously to Joe. "Let's go home, Joe. What do you say?"

"Okay," agrees Joe, only too happy to leave this scary place. "See you tomorrow."

Three nine-year-old boys heave three great sighs of relief as they turn away from the rattling shutters and peeling paint of the deserted house.

"Hi, fellers! Where you going?"

Sighs of relief become groans of dismay as they turn toward the unwelcome shout. "It's me!" calls Toby, pushing to them through the grass and weeds.

"Hi," he says as he reaches them at last.

"Hi," they answer, trying not to sound as unhappy as they feel.

"Hear any noises?"

"Lots of them," Harry says quickly, hoping to change Toby's mind.

"From inside the house?"

"Uh-huh," Mike says, hoping Toby will be too frightened to go in.

"Real scary noises, like chains and things," adds Joe.

Toby looks up at the house and gulps. Maybe this isn't such a good idea after all. Then he remembers the baseball game and the way they had laughed at him.

"I don't care if there are noises," he finally says. "I'm going in anyway." He points his flashlight at the cracked and weather-beaten door. "Come on."

Nobody moves but Toby. Harry and Mike are so frightened at the very thought of actually going into the old house that they can hardly think. All they can do is look at Joe and hope he will get them out of this.

By now Toby is at the front door, a small dark figure in the shadows. He glances toward them. "You coming?" he asks. "Or are you too scared?" He is staring directly at Joe, challenging him.

"Course I'm not scared," Joe says promptly, moving up alongside Toby.

"Me, either," say Harry and Mike, joining the other two at the front door.

The truth of the matter is that all four of them are frightened as Toby pushes against the door, and it slowly moves inward on screeching hinges. He steps into the musty dark living room, then stands aside to let the others enter.

Joe comes first. Then Harry and Mike. Wide-eyed, nervous, trembling with fear, the three Phantoms of the Fourth Grade walk into this house that hasn't been lived in since before they were born. Holding their flashlights tightly, they stare at the jumbled broken furniture and at the cobwebs hanging everywhere.

BANG! The front door slams shut!

All three jump at the sound. "Who did that?" gasps Harry.

"It wasn't a ghost," Toby says. "It was me."

"Can't we leave it open?" Joe suggests hopefully.

"No," says Toby firmly. "It has to be closed." He reaches up, grabs the bolt, and slams it shut.

They are alone. Four boys, locked in the stomach of the ogre. Somewhere a dog howls. Somewhere else a bullfrog croaks. Joe, Harry, and Mike huddle together, nervously eying the littered, shadowy, creaky, scary room. They wonder what will happen now.

Toby watches them, trying not to smile.

He *knows* what will happen now.

Chapter Nineteen: I'm coming up to get you!

The Phantoms of the Fourth Grade stand in the center of the cluttered living room, staring fearfully into every dark corner. With the door shut and bolted, the outside world seems a zillion miles away, and the bullfrog's croak sounds like the voice of doom.

They shine their flashlights, almost afraid of what they might see in this menacing, ghostly old house. The light bounces off cobwebs, filtering through the clouds of dust kicked up by their feet. They see the battered old fireplace, the scattered pieces of furniture, and the pile of cartons and empty crates stacked near the front door.

What they don't know is how long it took Toby to pile those crates and cartons just where he wanted them. And what they don't notice is the end of a rope sticking out from the bottom of the pile.

What they do notice is the spooky stairway leading up to the blackness of the second floor. "I'll bet that's where the ghosts are. Upstairs," whispers Harry.

"Yeah," says Mike. He shivers. "It's so dark in here."

"Yeah," agrees Joe. He looks at Toby, who is still standing near the front door. "How long we going to stay here?"

"I told you. Until midnight."

"But that's almost two hours," complains Harry.

"Do we have to?" moans Mike fearfully.

"Why?" demands Toby. "You scared?"

"Course not!" Mike says promptly.

"Who's scared?" says Harry.

"Not me!" says Joe.

That's what they say, but the way they look around, the way they shine their flashlights into the darkness, the way they jump at every creak of the floorboards under them shows how happy they would be to leave this place and never come back. But they can't do that without a good reason.

Joe thinks he has a reason. "Ghosts only come out when there's a full moon," he says to Harry and Mike. "There's no full moon tonight, so there won't be any ghosts. Maybe we should come back some other time."

"Yeah, next week maybe," Harry agrees eagerly.

"What do you say, Toby?" pleads Mike, turning to the spot where Toby had been standing. His eyes widen with terror. Harry gasps in fear. Joe stares in horror.

There's no sign of Toby! He's gone! Disappeared!

"Where is he?" whispers Mike.

"Where did he go?" moans Harry.

"What happened to him?" worries Joe.

They start calling, shouting Toby's name in the darkness, pointing their flashlights in all directions, too frightened to search in the corners for the missing boy.

"I bet the ghosts got him!" cries Mike, almost in tears.

"Toby! Toby, where are you!" shouts Joe.

"Toby! Toby!" yells Harry.

The three boys huddle together in fear in the center of the dark living room of the haunted house, calling Toby's name, not knowing that someone is watching every move they make.

That someone is Toby. Crouched in the darkness behind the pile of crates and cartons he had so carefully constructed the day before, he smiles at their terror and almost laughs out loud at their shouts. Then he reaches out and grabs the end of the rope protruding from under the crates and cartons.

He pulls!

CRASH! Down comes the pile of boxes. Down it comes with a crash and a roar and a crackle and a boom. Down it comes, tumbling to the floor, blocking the front door, slamming in the darkness like the rattle of a thousand hammers!

"Mama!" screams Mike.

"Help!" scream Harry and Joe.

Only one thought now. Out. They have to get out. They pull and they push and they tug and they scrabble, and they don't notice Toby sneaking through the shadows, crossing the dark room, bending down by the fireplace.

He looks over his shoulder. He sees the Phantoms of the Fourth Grade desperately trying to fight their way through the fallen crates and boxes. He reaches out into the fireplace and flips the switch on his tape recorder, hidden under a half-burned log. The tape begins to turn.

"EEEEEEEEEEEEEE!" screams the tape, repeating the scream Toby had shouted into it yesterday.

"EEEEEEEEEEEEEEE!" it shrieks in the darkness, making the three boys jump in terror.

"The ghost! It's the ghost!" yells Harry.

"Mama! I want my mama!" cries Mike.

"Hurry! Hurry!" shouts Joe, pushing crates and cartons out of the way as fast as he can.

The tape turns. The darkness is filled with hollow laughter and moans and the rattling of chains. "It's coming after us!" screams Joe, still not noticing Toby watching from the shadows, his hand over his mouth, trying to keep from laughing out loud.

The laughter and the screams and the rattles and the moans echo over and over in the musty room, and the sobbing, gasping, terrified boys struggle to escape.

"Upstairs!" Toby suddenly shouts, rushing out of the darkness, dashing up to them. "It's the only way!" They stare at him startled, wondering where he had come from. "Upstairs!" he shouts again. "Come on!"

Up the stairway Toby clatters, pretending to be as frightened as they are. Up the stairway stumble Harry, Mike, and Joe, feeling a ghost is going to jump on them any minute. Up the stairway float the screams, the laughs, the moans, the rattling of chains.

To the top of the dark landing they go, hearts pounding, breath gasping, eyes wide with fear, so terrified they don't even notice Toby reaching up to pull another rope.

CRASH! Down the stairway tumbles another pile of boxes, cartons, pieces of wood, lengths of chain, odds and ends of anything that can clatter and crash and frighten three boys almost to death.

"I want to go home!" screams Harry. "I want to go home!"

And then a strange voice is heard, the most frightening, hollow, ghostly voice any of them could imagine. "I'm coming up to get you," the voice calls out in the darkness.

"I'm coming up to get you!" the voice repeats, floating up from the tape recorder hidden in the fireplace.

"I'M COMING UP TO GET YOU!" the hollow voice cries out again, like an icy hand reaching from beyond the grave.

And then another sound! CLUMP-CLUMP-CLUMP! Footsteps! To the terrified boys, the sound of footsteps seems to be coming up the stairway.

"It's coming after us!" screams Joe in terror.

"It's going to get us!" cries Harry, not knowing which way to run.

CLUMP-CLUMP-CLUMP sound the footsteps.

"The attic!" shouts Toby. "Hurry!"

Along the landing he races, past closed doors and rotting walls, the three boys close at his heels. Up another stairway toward the attic they scramble, knees knocking, teeth chattering, hair almost standing on end.

Into the attic they rush, across the low-ceilinged room, knocking over a broken rocking horse and a rusted baby carriage as they dash for the only window.

Toby stays at the door. Slowly and quietly he closes it. Slowly and quietly he turns the key in the lock. Slowly and quietly he puts the key in his pocket.

He smiles. Everything is working out exactly as he had planned.

So far.

Chapter Twenty:
Trapped!

EEEEEEE! AAHHHHHHHH! OOOOOOOOOO! CLUMP!

From the stomach of the ogre come screams and moans and the menacing clomping of footsteps, filtering up through the wide cracks in the attic floor, terrifying the three boys who think they will be attacked by ghosts.

Near the locked door stands Toby, trying not to laugh as he watches the Phantoms of the Fourth Grade frantically clearing a path through the jumble of junk in the attic, desperately trying to reach the window before the clomping monster grabs them all.

Moan! Groan! Scream! Clomp! Joe Rooney's heart beats wildly as he pushes aside a rusted old bicycle, knocks away a bedspring, reaches the window, and looks down. Hopeless. He sees a narrow ledge about ten feet below. And that's all. Nothing else but the ground, far far down.

"We're trapped!" he cries. "We can't get out!"

"What'll we do?" Harry moans. "The ghost'll get us!"

"I want my mama!" sobs Mike.

EEEEEE! AAHHHHHHHH! OOOOOOOO! CLUMP!

Joe looks around desperately. "Maybe there's a rope up here. Maybe we can climb down."

"The ghost'll get us first! I know it!" screams Mike as another terrifying moan echoes from the darkness below.

And then they hear laughter. Not from down below, not from the stairway, not from outside, but from right there in the attic. Real laughter that makes them turn in greater fear than ever and stare at what they see.

What they see is Toby. Not only is Toby laughing, but he is laughing so hard that tears are coming to his eyes. He is laughing so hard that he is doubled over and sputtering and choking and seeming to be having such a good time that they all think he must have gone crazy.

"You think it's funny!" shouts Mike. "The ghost'll get us!"

"It'll kill us, Toby!" exclaims Joe. "It'll kill all of us!"

"What will?" sputters Toby, trying to laugh and talk at the same time. "My tape recorder?"

"What tape recorder?" says Joe.

"It's a ghost!" cries Harry. "A real ghost!"

"Creeps!" laughs Toby. "You're all creeps!"

"What tape recorder?" insists Joe.

"The one I hid in the fireplace. The one that's making all the noises." Toby starts to moan and groan and scream, sounding just like the noises he had recorded the day before. "I'm coming up to get you!" he says, in the same deep voice that had made them run in terror.

Joe stares at him, unable to believe it. "You made all those noises?"

Toby nods, laughing so hard again that he can't even talk this time.

"What about the boxes and everything?"

"I pulled them down with a rope," sputters Toby, trying to keep from laughing. He points a triumphant finger at the three Phantoms of the Fourth Grade. "Cry-babies!" he chortles. "Wait'll I tell them in class tomorrow! Just wait'll I tell them!"

The three boys look at each other in dismay and embarrassment. "You wouldn't dare," challenges Joe.

"Why not?" grins Toby. "You made them laugh at me. Now they'll all laugh at you." He starts laughing all over again, while Joe, Harry, and Mike stand there helplessly, wondering how they could have let this happen. How could they let Toby trick them? They can almost hear the rest of the kids laughing at them tomorrow when Toby tells about it.

But that's tomorrow. Right now, tonight, they're up here in the attic in the haunted house, and the only important thing is to get out. Mike rushes for the door and tries to open it.

"It's locked!" he cries. "Where's the key?"

"Right here," grins Toby, patting his pocket, enjoying every moment of this.

"Open the door, Toby," Mike pleads. "Please."

"Cry-baby."

"Make him open the door, Joe. I'm scared."

"That's because I'm smarter than you are," Toby chortles. He looks at Joe. "And all the baseball and bike riding and tree climbing in the world can't help you now."

"Get the key, Joe. Please," cries Mike, almost in tears.

Joe walks up to Toby and holds out his hand. "Give me the key, Toby," he says.

"No."

"Give it to me," Joe repeats.

"No, I won't."

"Yes, you will!" shouts Joe, jumping for Toby and trying to pull the key from his pocket. Down they go, down onto the dusty floor of the attic, rolling over and over in the darkness as the other two boys watch anxiously.

"Get the key, Joe!" yells Harry.

"Get it from him!" screams Mike.

Scratching, pulling, punching, rolling through a pile of wire hangers, knocking against an old headboard, falling into cobwebs and rusty tools, Toby and Joe struggle while Harry and Mike shout and holler and pray that Joe will get the key.

Into Toby's pocket goes Joe's hand. Rip goes the pocket. Clink goes the key as it falls to the floor. Reach goes Toby, trying to get it back. Push goes Joe, knocking Toby away. Stretch goes Toby, trying to get the key before Joe picks it up.

Clink, stretch, push, shove, reach, with the key being knocked closer and closer to a big hole in the floor. Closer and closer it goes, every time Joe or Toby try to pick it up. Closer and closer, until Toby touches it, moves it a little, and sees it fall through the hole!

Clunk! They can all hear the sound as the precious key hits the floor of the room below.

Clunk! Toby and Joe stop struggling and stare at the hole in the floor. The key is gone. They can never reach it now. Mike sobs, Harry moans, and Joe looks angrily at Toby.

Suddenly Toby dashes for the door, desperate, anxious, fearful. He pulls and he tugs and he struggles, but the door won't open. Terrified now, he turns and stares at the three boys he had been laughing at such a short time ago.

The door is locked. The Phantoms of the Fourth Grade are trapped in the attic of the old deserted house.

And Toby is trapped with them.

Chapter Twenty-one:
Help! Somebody help!

The attic is a jumble sitting on an ogre and surrounded by blackness. It is a junk pile balanced on terror and hemmed in by fear. It is a prison resting on nowhere and bordered by noplace.

It is a catalogue of years long forgotten, filled with bits and pieces of lives long gone. Cartons of discarded junk sit on its dusty floor. Boxes of memories pile in its corners. Broken mirrors, rusted bicycles, bed springs, headboards, wire hangers, bed slats, rocking horses, baby carriages, rusty tools, doorknobs, old newspapers, and dozens of remnants of other days lie scattered under its creaking, groaning, cobwebbed roof.

Outside a dog howls, a long, drawn-out, mournful sound in the night. In the fireplace far below, the tape recorder is silent at last. Nothing moves but a tiny field mouse, scampering among the cartons and crates that still block the front door.

Toby sits on the floor of the attic, frightened and unhappy. He stares at the boards beneath him, wondering why nothing ever works out the way he plans. He had everything figured out so perfectly. Why did it have to go wrong? Why?

Under the useless window sits Harry, thinking of ghosts and goblins, wondering when his mother and father will miss him. Probably not until morning, he thinks, and by then we'll all be dead.

Pressed close to Harry crouches Mike, sniffling a little as he tries to hold back his tears. No one ever goes near this old house but us, he thinks, and no one will ever find us. If the ghosts don't get us, we'll starve to death. A lonely tear rolls down his cheek.

Squatting near one of the broken bicycles is Joe, thinking of how worried his grandfather will be. We can't be trapped in here forever, he thinks. There must be some way to get out. His jaw sets with determination, he flicks on his flashlight and rises.

The others watch Joe silently as he pokes around in the boxes and cartons, searches in corners, looks through piles of newspapers and the odds and ends of bits and pieces surrounding them.

"What are you looking for?" Harry finally asks.

"A rope. With all this junk, there ought to be a piece of rope somewhere."

"There is no rope," Toby says.

"How do you know?"

"Because I made sure yesterday. I found a rope, and I threw it out the window."

"Why?"

"So you'd all be good and scared, that's why."

"That's what you get for being so smart."

"How should I know we'd all be stuck up here?"

Toby and Joe glare angrily at each other through the menacing shadows. Somewhere, a shutter bangs against the

side of the old house. An owl hoots. A cat screams. A floor-board creaks. Joe and Toby stare furiously into each other's eyes, and this time neither of them feels like giggling.

Harry buries his face in his hands. "We'll never get out," he moans. "We're really stuck."

Mike points an accusing finger at Toby. "It's all his fault!" he cries.

"It is not!" Toby retorts. "It's Joe's fault! He pulled the key out of my pocket, didn't he?"

"I don't care!" shouts Mike, jumping to his feet. "I want to go home!" He rushes to the window, leans out as far as he can, and starts to scream. "Help!" he yells. "Somebody help!"

A mad rush of feet as the other three boys join Mike at the window, crowding around him, pushing, shoving, each one desperate and frightened and frantic to escape.

"Help!" they all scream. "Somebody help! We're up here! Help!"

The shouts float through the night, over the deserted meadow, through the brambles and rye grass and weeds, over the rickety wooden bridge, into the darkness.

"Help! Somebody help!" they call over and over again.

Nobody hears.

Nobody answers.

Chapter Twenty-two:
Toby has an idea

Midnight. The witching hour. The time of goblins, vampires, ghosts, and unseen terrors in the night. The time when every rustle and creak seems like approaching horror to four small boys trapped in an attic.

Two hours have passed and nothing has changed. The old house still sits in the deserted meadow. The creek still flows under the wooden bridge. Dark clouds still hide the sliver of a moon. And the town of Carlyle is fast asleep.

Toby's mother and father lie in their beds, breathing gently. Joe's grandfather snores. Harry's parents smile and dream of happy hours. Mike's mother and father rest quietly as curtains sway in the cool October night.

In the attic, the long minutes tick by on an endless chain of fear. Tick-tick-tick. The four boys sit hopelessly on the floor, wondering if the night will ever pass. Tick-tick-tick. Toby wishes, for the twentieth time, he had never tried to show how smart he was. Tick-tick-tick. Joe wishes, for the fiftieth time, he had never laughed at a boy who couldn't play baseball. Tick-tick-tick. Harry and Mike wish, for the hundreth time, they were safe in their own beds.

"Maybe we should yell some more," Mike suggests.

"It's no use," Joe answers. "Nobody can hear us."

They sit in silence, staring helplessly at the floor. Darkness presses in on them like the walls of a prison. Loneliness engulfs them like a vast empty ocean. Fear surrounds them like a hungry, unearthly monster.

Then they hear it. A sound. A tiny sound at first, but then it grows louder. It seems to come from over their heads.

"What's that?" Toby asks fearfully, looking up toward the attic ceiling.

"I don't know," gasps Harry, almost too frightened to talk.

The four boys follow the sound with terror-filled eyes as it moves across the ceiling, scrabbling along like little claws. It moves slowly from one side to the other.

"I don't see anything," whispers Joe. "Do you?"

"No," whispers Toby.

"Maybe it's only a squirrel on the roof."

"Maybe it's a ghost," shudders Toby as he watches the ceiling.

"I thought you didn't believe in ghosts," says Joe.

"Maybe I was wrong," says Toby, expecting to see a terrible figure appear on the ceiling at any moment.

Back and forth the strange sound goes, back and forth, from one side of the rafters to the other. Back and forth their eyes go, watching it, waiting breathlessly, wondering how they would escape if a monster should appear.

It stops. As quickly as it had started, it stops.

They wait, still watching the ceiling, still expecting terror to leap among them. Tick-tick-tick. Waiting-waiting-waiting. Suddenly, Mike crumples to the floor and starts to sob helplessly.

"Don't cry, Mike," Joe says. "Whatever it was, it's gone."

"I don't care," Mike sobs. "I'm scared."

"It was only a squirrel," Toby says, wanting to comfort him. "I'm sure that's all it was."

"I don't care," Mike cries, shoulders shaking, tears rolling down his cheeks. "We're going to die. No one's ever going to find us."

He sobs pitifully, no longer a baseball player or a bike rider or even a reluctant ghost hunter. At this moment he is nothing more than a frightened nine-year-old boy.

"We're going to die," he sobs. "We're going to die."

"No, we're not," Joe answers firmly, turning to Toby, eyes blazing with fury. "You got us into this!" he says angrily. "You're supposed to be so smart! Why don't *you* figure a way out!"

"What do you expect me to do?" Toby retorts just as angrily. He jumps up and points at the collection of junk in the attic. "Do you expect me to make a rope out of a baby carriage or a rocking horse or some ratty old bicycles or some boxes full of . . ."

He stops talking in the middle of his sentence. In fact, he stops so quickly that they all stare at him.

"What is it?" asks Harry.

"Did you hear something?" asks Joe.

"I thought of something," answers Toby, his eyes bright the way they always are when he thinks of a good idea. "I thought of a way we might be able to make a rope."

"How?" they all exclaim.

Toby doesn't answer. Instead, he walks across the attic and bends down beside one of the rusted and broken bicycles. Humming a song no one ever heard before, he examines the wheels and the spokes and the nuts and the bolts, while the other three boys watch him, wondering what he plans to do.

"Come on, Toby," Joe finally says. "How do you expect to make a rope out of a broken old bicycle?"

"Even a genius couldn't do that," remarks Harry.

"We're all going to die," sobs Mike.

Toby pays no attention to them at all. He keeps studying the bicycle, humming all the while. Finally he turns to Joe. "There are some old tools in that corner," he says. "Bring them over."

"What for?" Joe wants to know.

"Never mind. Just get them." Toby turns to Mike. "I saw some wire hangers up here. Find them." Then he has some instructions for Harry. "Find a piece of strong wood wider than the window. A bed slat, maybe."

Joe, Harry, and Mike jump up quickly, eager to do anything that might help them escape from this horrible, frightening place. They can't imagine how anybody could expect to make a rope out of bicycles and wire hangers and bed slats, but if Toby is as good at inventing as he is in geography and history and arithmetic, maybe he *can* do it.

Joe finds the tools. Mike finds the wire hangers. Harry finds a bed slat. Still puzzled, they bring them to Toby, who is concentrating on the bicycle.

"I'll need the wrench," he tells Joe. "Mike will need the pliers and the wire cutters." Turning to Mike, he says, "Use the pliers to take some wire hangers apart. Then use the wire cutters to cut them into six-inch pieces."

"What do I do with the bed slat?" asks Harry.

"Hold it," answers Toby, "until I'm ready for it."

He takes the wrench from Joe, bends down alongside the bicycle, and starts to take it apart.

Chapter Twenty-three:
Toby, the inventor!

Silence. Only the heavy breathing of three boys as they watch Toby anxiously. Only the scraping of a wrench as Toby removes one bolt after another from the rusted bicycle.

Off comes the rear wheel. Off come the pedals. Off come this bolt and that bolt, this pin and that pin. Off comes the loop of chain that connects the pedal to the rear wheel.

"This is known as a drive chain," Toby says, holding the loop in his hand.

"We know that," says Mike impatiently, anxious to know what Toby has in mind.

"Now watch carefully," Toby announces, trying to sound like a professor conducting an experiment.

Taking the pliers from Mike, he grips one link of the drive chain and twists. He twists and bends and bends and twists, until he breaks the link. The loop comes apart and is now a four-foot-long metal chain dangling from his hand.

"Eureka!" he cries, the way inventors often do. "What was once a drive chain is now a rope!"

"But it's not long enough," complains Harry.

"Correct," agrees Toby. "But if we take the chains off the other two bikes, and tie them all together with the strips Mike cut from the metal hangers, then we'll have a twelve-foot rope." He grins, adding, "And that is certainly long enough."

The Phantoms of the Fourth Grade look at the chain, look at Toby, look at each other, and suddenly explode with excitement and joy.

"Toby, you're a genius!" shouts Joe, flinging his arms in the air and doing a dance.

"It'll work! It'll work!" yells Harry, spinning around and around almost dropping the bed slat.

"How did you ever figure it out!" screams Mike, jumping up and down until his glasses fall off his nose.

They dance and they jump and they shout and they pound Toby on the back and then they dance some more. They scream and they whirl and they sing and they tell Toby what a genius he is.

"What about the bed slat?" Harry finally asks when he catches his breath. "What's that for?"

"I'll show you," answers Toby, still grinning at their praise. "First we have to get the drive chains off the other two bikes."

He sets to work again, removing bolts and pins and wheels and pedals, until he has two more drive chains in his hands. Twist of the pliers. Another twist. Two more four-foot lengths of chain.

"Yayyy!" yell the Phantoms of the Fourth Grade.

Taking the strips Mike had cut from the wire hangers, Toby twists them carefully and tightly through the end link of one chain into the end link of another, until all the chains are tied securely together into one long twelve-foot escape from fear.

"Ahhhh!" sigh the Phantoms of the Fourth Grade.

"That should be long enough to reach the ledge," Toby says proudly.

"What keeps it from falling out the window?" asks Joe with concern.

"That's what the bed slat is for," answers Toby, taking the long piece of stout wood from Harry. "The bed slat is wider than the window, right?"

"Right," they all answer.

"So if we put it across the window, it can't fall through, right?"

"Right!"

"And if we tie the chain around the middle of the bed slat and then put the bed slat across the window, the chain can't fall either, right?"

"RIGHT!"

More cheers. More jumping. More praise. More grins. Within minutes, Toby has tied the chain around the bed slat, fastening it securely with another strip from a wire hanger. The attic no longer seems so scary as he carries the bed slat toward the window, the chain trailing along the floor behind him.

Carefully, he props the strip of wood across the narrow window. Carefully, he lowers the chain, letting it fall as far as 'it will go. Quickly, Joe and Harry lean out over the window sill.

"It reaches the ledge," grins Harry.

"And look!" says Joe, pointing to one side. "There's a trellis about fifteen feet away. All we have to do is climb down to the ledge, crawl over to the trellis, and we can get down easy."

"Toby, the inventor!" cries Mike, so happy he can hardly stand still.

"Who goes first?" Harry asks.

"Me," answers Mike promptly. "I'll go first."

"That's not fair," Joe says. "It's Toby's invention. He should go first." He grins at Toby. "Go ahead. It's easy."

For the first time since he thought of his idea, Toby is beginning to feel a little nervous as he moves slowly toward the window. It's one thing to invent a rope out of bicycle chains and wire coat hangers and a bed slat, but it's another thing to climb out of a window to a narrow ledge twenty feet above the ground. He hopes they don't notice how much he is shaking as he pulls himself up onto the window sill.

"Toby, the inventor!" Mike shouts again, trying to sound like a circus announcer. "First man out of the haunted house! Tara!"

"Tara!" echo Joe and Harry, like trumpets in a big brass band.

Toby tries to smile. It isn't much of a smile. He is far too busy holding his breath as he looks over the edge of the window.

He sees the chain dangling down to the ledge ten feet below, a ledge that looks as if it's at least a thousand feet away. He sees the ground beneath it, far far down, with the grass and the weeds and the brambles seeming to twist and turn and tell him he will fall.

He feels more fear and terror than he has ever known in his life. His legs wobble, his body shakes, his hands are cold and clammy.

"I can't do it!" he suddenly screams, scrambling back into the attic. "I can't do it!"

"Why not?" asks Joe, startled by Toby's unexpected shout. "It's easy."

"I'll fall!" wails Toby. "I'll get dizzy and I'll fall! I know it! I know it!"

"No, you won't," Joe assures him. "All you have to do is grab the chain and let yourself down slowly."

"Leave me alone!" Toby cries. "Leave me alone! I'm not going! I don't care what you say! I'm not going out that window!"

He turns away suddenly, sits down against the wall, and crouches there, not looking at any of them. His heart is pounding, his head is dizzy, his eyes stare wildly at the floor.

His whole body shakes with fear.

Chapter Twenty-four:
I'm a creep

Solid as a rock, frozen as a swimming hole in winter, still as a frog waiting for a fly, Toby crouches against the wall of the attic, staring down at the floor, wishing he were dead.

I must really be a creep, he thinks. Who else but a creep would be too frightened to climb down that chain? What good does it do me to be smart enough to invent a rope if I'm too scared to use it?

He's sure the other boys are ready to laugh at him again, ready to call him names and make fun of him. And the worst thing about it is that he wouldn't blame them this time.

"Go ahead," he hears Joe say to Mike.

Over the window sill Mike scrambles, down the chain he slides, plop on the ledge he lands. Holding himself flat against the side of the house, he edges along the narrow ledge until he reaches the weather-beaten ivy trellis. Down the trellis he climbs toward freedom, grinning every step of the way.

"He made it, Joe!" shouts Harry, leaning out the window to watch. "He made it!"

Joe looks at Toby crouched in the shadows, wants to say something but doesn't know what to say. Instead, he turns to Harry and says, "Go ahead. You next."

Harry is even faster than Mike as he slides down the chain, edges along the ledge, and scrambles down the trellis. In less than two minutes, Mike is calling up from below. "He made it, Joe!" he yells. "Come on!"

Joe stands at the attic window, thinking hard. Ahead of him is the chain rope and freedom. Behind him is a frightened boy, trembling in the darkness. It's not my fault, Joe thinks. I can't help it if he's too scared to do an easy thing like slide down a chain.

"Come on, Joe!" Harry calls from below. "What are you waiting for?"

Joe climbs up onto the window sill. Far below, he can see Harry and Mike safe on the ground, looking up, waiting. It's an easy climb, he thinks. If Toby wasn't such a creep, he would be home and in bed in ten minutes.

"Let's go, Joe!" shouts Mike.

"Come on!" yells Harry.

Joe swings around, so he can go out the window backward and slide down the chain. He can look into the attic now. He can see parts of bicycles where Toby had left them. He can see bits of wire coat hangers. He can see bed slats in the corner. Most of all, he can see the boy who had been smart enough to put those pieces together and make a rope for all of them.

"Hurry up, Joe!" call Harry and Mike. "We want to get home!"

Joe doesn't move. He perches on the window sill, thinking harder than he ever did in his life. I can't invent a rope, he thinks, but Toby can. Toby can't climb down it, but I can. And if Toby's a creep for not being able to climb down a rope, then maybe I'm a creep for not being able to invent one.

Or maybe none of us are creeps, he thinks. Maybe we're just different from each other, that's all.

All of this goes around and around in his brain while he perches on the window sill, while Harry and Mike are yelling for him to hurry. It's a lot of thinking for a nine-year-old boy at one in the morning in a haunted house, but it's probably the most important thinking that Joe has ever done in his life.

Toby crouches on the floor, against the wall, eyes tightly closed, feeling sad and lonely and afraid. Feeling lost and deserted and forlorn. Feeling a snake running around in his stomach.

"Toby . . ."

He looks up, surprised to see Joe standing beside him.

"I know," Toby says sadly. "I'm a creep."

"No, you're not. Come on. I'll help you down."

"How?"

"I'll go first, and I'll wait for you on the ledge. I won't let you fall. I promise."

Without even waiting for an answer, Joe walks back to the window, hops back up on the window sill, swings around to face the room, and sees that Toby hasn't moved. "Come on," he says.

Slowly, fearfully, Toby rises and approaches Joe. "I'll never make it, Joe," he says.

"Sure you will," Joe replies reassuringly. In an instant he has disappeared out the window, down the chain, and onto the ledge. Gripping a protruding shingle with one hand, he shouts, "Okay, Toby! I'm ready!"

The worst tasting medicine his mother had ever given him never made him feel as sick as forcing himself up onto the window sill. The fastest roller coaster in Coney Island never made him as dizzy as looking down and seeing Joe perched on the ledge waiting for him to slide down the chain.

I'll fall, he thinks. I know I'll fall, and I'll knock Joe down with me.

"Come on, Toby!" Joe calls. "You can make it!"

No time to think. Toby reaches out, grips the chain tightly, closes his eyes, and slides!

Chapter Twenty-five:
Am I glad
you're smart!

Down. Down into emptiness. Down a twelve-foot chain that feels a million miles long. Down a chain that stings and burns your hands. Down a chain that ends at a narrow ledge far above the ground.

Down he goes, hitting the ledge with both feet, legs buckling, swaying, about to fall. Out reaches an arm, gripping him tightly, pulling, forcing him back against the side of the house.

In his ears a reassuring voice. "You're okay, Toby. You're okay. Just hold on."

Trembling with fear, Toby opens his eyes. The peeling paint of the old house is not more than an inch away from his face. Beside him, Joe still clings to a shingle as he tries to steady Toby on the narrow ledge.

"Don't look down, whatever you do," Joe cautions. Toby nods, too frightened to speak. "I'm going to let go of the shingle now," Joe continues, "and then we're going to start moving to the trellis."

"I'll fall," Toby whispers hoarsely.

"No, you won't," Joe assures him. "Not if you move slowly and stay close to the wall of the house."

Down below, Harry and Mike, watching anxiously. On the ledge, Toby and Joe, starting to inch slowly toward the ivy trellis. High above, clouds drifting away and the moon casting a faint glimmer of light on their goal, only fifteen feet away.

Fifteen feet. Fifteen endless feet of shuffling, gripping shingles, swaying, trembling. A shingle pulls away in Toby's grasp and he starts to teeter. Joe reaches out quickly, pushes him back to momentary safety. Toby presses his body hard against the wall of the old house, rigid, frozen in fear.

"I can't go any further," he moans.

"Yes, you can," Joe hisses. "Only ten feet more." He moves on without waiting.

Gritting his teeth, terrified of being left alone on the ledge, Toby inches along, feeling the wind on his face, the emptiness at his back, shivering and shaking and sure he will fall.

Five feet more, then three. Then the wonderful, marvelous, joyful moment when he reaches the trellis!

Joe is there, hanging on, waiting to help Toby, eyes shining, mouth split in a Halloween grin.

"We made it!" he exults, stepping onto the trellis and guiding Toby's feet to the wooden slats that form a pathway to the ground.

"We made it!" echoes Toby, sighing with relief as he grips the framework of the trellis with both hands.

"Come on!" shouts Joe happily.

Down the trellis he scrambles. Down climbs Toby, close behind. Down they come, Joe landing lightly on his feet, Toby slipping, sliding, tumbling the last few feet, hitting the ground with a clomp, rolling over and over, and hopping up again like a smiling yo-yo.

"You okay, Toby?" asks Harry, rushing over to help him up.

"You all right?" asks Mike, dashing over to brush him off.

"Super!" shouts Toby, grinning as if he had never grinned before.

"Hurray for the hero!" shouts Harry, raising Joe's arm high in the air. "He saved the inventor!"

"Hurray for the inventor!" shouts Mike, raising Toby's arm as high as it would go. "He saved all of us!"

"Hurray for us!" they all shout, without worrying about baseball or chess or bike riding or arithmetic or tree climbing or Geiger counters or anything that makes one boy different from another.

"Hey, it's late. We'd better get home," Mike finally says.

"Yeah," agrees Harry. "See you in school tomorrow, fellers."

"See you," answer Toby and Joe, as the other two boys hurry off through the darkness to homes they had thought they would never see again.

Two boys stand alone in front of an old deserted house. Two boys who have been through an adventure they will never forget. Two boys who have fought and laughed and struggled and shivered until a narrow path had become wide enough for both of them.

"I sure was scared," Toby says, looking up at the dark hulk of a house looming before him.

"Me, too," says Joe, remembering the long hours they had been trapped in the attic. Then he looks at Toby. "Boy, am I glad you're smart!"

"Am I glad you're strong!" They smile at each other. Then Toby bends down suddenly, picks up two stones, and hands one to Joe. "Ready?" he asks.

"Yeah," smiles Joe.

Together, they look at the haunted house. Together, they raise their arms. Together, they shout, "Come on out, ghosts! Come on out!"

Clatter go the stones against the peeling paint of the walls that had held them prisoner. Scramble go the two boys, running through the meadow. Whistle goes the wind through the tall grass and the weeds.

Laughing, scampering, giggling, shouting, tumbling, rolling over and over in the brambles, helping each other up, forgetting their yesterdays, chasing after their tomorrows, Toby and Joe zoom through the night like twin rockets heading straight for the moon.

Toby has never been so happy in his life.

ART WALLACE, a native of Brooklyn, was graduated from the City College of New York. A highly regarded and prolific writer and producer for television, his output has varied from scripts for *The Bill Cosby Show* and the TV movie *Dr. Cook's Garden*, starring Bing Crosby, to the creation of the spooky and successful daytime serial, *Dark Shadows*. While under contract to Twentieth Century-Fox as a TV producer, he produced *Hong Kong* and *Adventures in Paradise*. He is an avaricious traveler who drives his wife mad with his consuming curiosity about people and places. He and his artist wife, Soni, and their teen-age daughter, Sheila, combine the best of two worlds by dividing their time between New York City and their seven acre home in Newtown, Connecticut.